Trembling, she searched for something intelli-gent to say. "Who are you?"

He tucked her arm into his, turned, and began to walk along the street toward her parents' rented town house. "Promise you will never again venture into the city alone at night."

Regret pricked her conscience. "I was foolish to behave thus. I *am* a lady. You must believe me!"

Once more he exclaimed something indecipherable in French, and he slowed his pace. "I doubt not your purity of heart."

"What may I call you? I am Georgette Talbot."

"I know." His voice was quiet. "Did you like the dog?"

"The dog? Caramel! You gave him to me? But, why? Who are you? Where have we met?" All too soon, she recognized the brick town houses and storefronts of Broad Street. Had her parents noticed her absence?

"Your dog, he will remind, each time you look at him, that your devoted slave worships the earth beneath your feet. *Nuit et jour,* I dream of you."

Georgette felt as though her feet floated above the paving stones.

He stopped at the garden gate and released her hand. "Carriages still wait out front. You might yet slip inside unnoted."

"You are leaving? Will you not come inside? I wish to see your face."

He backed away. She caught the edge of his cloak. "Will I meet you again?"

"Assuredly, yes."

JILL STENGL lives in the Northwoods of Wisconsin with her husband Dean, two of their four children (the oldest two are in college), three spoiled cats, and one sadly outnumbered dog. She enjoys writing fiction that portrays God's involvement in the lives of everyday people throughout history.

Books by Jill Stengl

HEARTSONG PRESENTS

HP197—Eagle Pilot
HP222—Finally, Love
HP292—A Child of Promise
HP335—Time for a Miracle
HP387—Grant Me Mercy
HP431—Myles from Anywhere

Faithful Traitor

Jill Stengl

Heartsong Presents

Dedicated with thanks to my invaluable critique partners, Beverly Olojan, Kim Vogel Sawyer, and Eileen Key.

And to Tom, who always wanted his mom to write a war book. Guess this one will have to do for now.

A note from the Author:
I love to hear from my readers! You may correspond with me by writing:

Jill Stengl
Author Relations
PO Box 719
Uhrichsville, OH 44683

ISBN 1-59310-331-X

FAITHFUL TRAITOR

Our mission is to publish and distribute inspirational products offering exceptional value and biblical encouragement to the masses.

All Scripture quotations are taken from the King James Version of the Bible.

PRINTED IN THE U.S.A.

Or check out our Web site at www.heartsongpresents.com

one

A good name is rather to be chosen than great riches,
and loving favour rather than silver and gold.
PROVERBS 22:1

October 1774

"How does it look, Mummy?" Georgette Talbot turned before her mirror and touched the strand of matched pearls adorning her throat. The snowy skirt drifted about her slippers. "I hardly recognize myself. Are you certain the bodice is not too daring? I should hate to be the subject of gossip tomorrow. You know how Marianne's mother is."

"Victoria Grenville can only dream of having a daughter as fair as either of my two treasures. Should anyone criticize your attire, 'twould be a matter of sour grapes. You have superb shoulders and flawless skin—we must emphasize them."

"Since my face is plain," Georgette completed the thought. "If only I were beautiful like you." She covered her mouth with one hand, holding up her elbow with the other.

"Bosh." Her mother studied her with a critical eye. "Stop covering your lips; it appears ill-bred. You are far from plain, as I have told you countless times. A discerning man will admire your excellent teeth, shapely figure, and golden hair."

"If that is true, my world is bereft of discerning men. They take one look at my colossal mouth and back away."

"It is not the *size* of your mouth that frightens men away, Georgette." Her mother's blue eyes held a warning. "Perhaps a touch more powder, Agnes. Her cheeks are too red. Is that as tight as you can make her stays?"

"Yes, madam," the maid said.

"Any tighter and I should swoon during the first dance." Georgette felt like a feather pillow with a cord tied about its middle. Her inward parts must be entirely disarranged.

But at least her waist was tiny.

Georgette's mother huffed. "You must trust your mother with these things, Georgette. Remember how successful your sister was in her debut—she had Mr. Honeywell enthralled almost from the moment she entered the ballroom, and now look at her, happily wedded to a rising barrister."

"But I am twenty now and no debutante, Mummy. There are no Mr. Honeywells here in New York. If ever I am to have opportunity to wed, we must return to England soon." She gazed through her dormer window at the tall merchant ships anchored in the river. "Please, can we not sail on one of those ships? I should die if we were to spend another summer in this hot, stinking village that calls itself a city!"

Her mother directed the maid to rearrange her skirts, then stood back to judge the effect. "You will marry whomever your parents approve for you, Georgette. You must allow that Juliette is happy, and she scarcely knew Mr. Honeywell on their wedding day. I had not intended to tell you this yet, but your papa has already selected a suitor—a discerning man—who can support you in a manner even superior to the one you now enjoy." She adjusted her own golden cloud of hair while looking into Georgette's mirror.

"Surely you do not mean that Mr. LaTournay he constantly talks about." Georgette lifted one brow.

"I do. The man is charming, influential in city politics, and wealthy enough to make him the target of every matchmaking mother in town."

"Ha! As if such a man would form an attachment to me."

"Indeed, Mr. LaTournay craves an introduction, and your father is of the opinion that the man has admired you for some time."

Mr. LaTournay had been watching her? Georgette reached for her throat and struggled to swallow. "But, Mother, his reputation!"

"I would discount much of the gossip you hear. Every man worth his salt sows a few wild oats before he settles down. You must not hold that against Mr. LaTournay. Is he not exceedingly handsome?"

"I have never met the man, Mummy, and I never wish to."

Her mother turned with a sweep of her skirts. "Come now. Your father has the carriage waiting."

Georgette drifted down the steep staircase with her gloved fingers skimming the handrail. Her anticipation of the dance had all but vanished. How often had she seen young women whisper behind their fans, cast fatuous glances at Mr. LaTournay's elegant figure, and burst into giggles?

"Georgette, do hurry!" Her father's call rattled the rafters.

❧

From their vantage point near the punch bowl, Georgette and her friend watched dancers spin and promenade across the floor. "I dislike sounding critical, but I believe the Harrisons invited too many ladies for the number of men tonight." To Georgette's relief, Mr. LaTournay seemed to be absent. Once when she spotted a tall man amid the throng, her heart had leaped to her throat, but the alarm proved false.

"There are few eligible men in town since this dreadful rebellion." Marianne Grenville fanned herself. "We must keep praying that the governor will return to the province and set things right. He has been away for months."

"Politics! I despise them. All this talk about the onset of anarchy. I should think any man of courage would refuse to put up with such nonsense." Georgette fluffed her skirts. "And as long as gaming tables remain open, my father is unlikely to take Mother and me back home to England. He says it is business that keeps him in town, but I know better. Marianne, if ever I am tempted to wed a gamester, please kick me."

"Surely it is not so bad as that."

"Surely it is. You may wish to believe ill of no one, my dear, but in this case thinking the worst is warranted." Georgette tried to sound indifferent. "My mother prattles about the importance of my making a brilliant match. As though any man would notice me when there are many local beauties of family and fortune for the asking. Such as you, for instance." She tapped her friend on the arm, smiling lest Marianne take offense.

"You are beautiful, Gigi, though not in the conventional way."

"So my mother tells me. And what precisely does that mean? Never mind; I think I should rather not know. It is certain that my style of beauty is not one to inspire sonnets and duels." She paused. "Not that I care for either."

Marianne blinked and attempted a smile. Dearly though Georgette loved her, Marianne would benefit from a dash more humor and romance amid her charms. "Someday, somewhere, you will meet the man you should marry, Gigi."

"Oh, Marianne, I fear that the man of my dreams does not exist. Is there a man yet living in this world who will love only one woman all his life?" Closing her eyes, Georgette clutched her fan to her chest and inhaled deeply, releasing her breath in a sigh. "I would make that man happier than he could imagine, if only he would love me for myself. Do you never dream of such love?"

Marianne's blue eyes expressed shock. "I try not to dwell on things of that sort, Gigi."

Georgette's shoulders drooped. "Perhaps it is not beneficial to dream, but at times dreams are my only escape. Reality is distressingly prosaic. Perhaps I should aspire to the stage."

Marianne glanced away. "I know you grow tired of hearing this, Gigi, but your burdens would seem much lighter if you would share them with God. He cares about your troubles and would help if you—"

"I know." Georgette crossed her arms over her chest in unladylike fashion. Her whalebone stays pinched. "I do think about what you tell me, Marianne. Truly, I do. Sometimes I feel God's presence and I want to believe, but it is all so strange. . . ."

Marianne touched her arm. "Here comes your father."

Frederick Talbot strode toward them, appearing strangely pleased. "LaTournay, I have been looking everywhere for you." His eyes focused beyond the two startled girls. "Have you and Georgette already been introduced?"

"I have not yet had the pleasure." The calm reply came from directly behind Georgette. Her blood congealed. Uncrossing her arms, she hurriedly looked down to make sure nothing was showing that oughtn't, then met her father's hopeful gaze.

"In that case, Georgette, please allow me to introduce Mr. LaTournay," he said. "He and I have conducted business for several years, though only recently have we met in person. He and his grandfather before him have been our best suppliers of fine wool. Mr. LaTournay, my daughter Georgette."

Murmuring something polite and keeping her eyes lowered, Georgette turned and extended her hand. Long fingers squeezed hers. A kiss tickled her hand as the man bowed with continental elegance. Brown hair had been brushed back from his high forehead into a neat pigtail. He spoke quietly. "Miss Talbot, will you honor me with your next dance?"

Georgette glanced at her father, who nodded. "I. . .yes." Mr. LaTournay lifted his head and met her gaze. She jerked her hand from his grasp and placed it over her heart. To her horror, his dark eyes followed the motion before he quickly looked away. Even after her father introduced LaTournay to Marianne, Georgette trembled in reaction. Instead of lilting violins, she heard blood pounding in her ears.

The men moved away. Georgette dragged her gaze from the back of LaTournay's emerald velvet coat and stared at the floor, struggling to check her scrambled thoughts and emotions.

"We have actually been introduced to Mr. LaTournay—and he asked you to dance!" Marianne said. "My mother says he is one of the most eligible bachelors in the entire colony. He is acquainted with Governor Tryon and with, oh, everyone of importance."

Georgette recovered her voice. "I care nothing for his connections. When he looked into my eyes, I felt. . ." Her vocabulary failed. "He has a huge mole on his face, and he wears a *beard.* Why would Papa wish me to know such a person?"

Marianne waved her fan before Georgette's eyes. "Many pardons, but do we speak of the same man? Mr. LaTournay is far from ugly. It is true that he seldom smiles, and his manners are somewhat stiff, but you could make him smile if anyone could, Gigi. He is a man with a great future, my father says."

"And a wicked past." Georgette rubbed her arms. "As if Apollyon himself took the form of a man. I do not wish to dance with him. I would rather stand here all evening than allow that fiend to touch my hand again." She backed up toward the wall.

Following, Marianne shook her head. "You are allowing imagination to nullify discretion. Just dance, Gigi. You will probably never see him again. Keep in mind that he has honored you with his request, and relax."

"I wonder how much of our conversation he overheard. He was standing behind us, Marianne, eavesdropping."

"Did we speak of anything shocking? Gigi—"

A British officer approached Marianne to request a dance. She accepted, fluttering her fan, leaving Georgette alone. With vague thoughts of escape, Georgette turned and bumped into LaTournay's brocaded waistcoat. Heat enflamed her body and face.

"Miss Talbot." He bowed and extended his arm.

Forcing herself to smile, she placed her hand on his velvet sleeve, and he led her to the dance floor. The musicians struck up a lively country-dance tune. Although her feet performed the dance steps, Georgette's mind went blank. Her careful training in the art of conversation was for naught.

Other couples chatted throughout the dance. Georgette and her partner remained silent. Crazed imaginings flitted through her mind. Sometimes women allowed men to escort them into the gardens. What would she do if Mr. LaTournay suggested such a move? Scream?

"How tragic that I have conducted business with your father these many years and never before met you."

His comment startled her into missing a step. He guided her back into place. Before she could reply, he continued. "Instead of bemoaning my loss, I should take pleasure in the moment. New York is privileged to have you, Miss Talbot, and I am delighted to make your acquaintance."

She avoided his eyes. "Although my father has traveled to these American colonies numerous times, my mother and I first arrived in this province with the trade ships last April. I know of you by repute."

"My usual practice is to summer in the country and return to town for trade with foreign merchants," he said. "Winter will soon be upon us, so I must return north before the river becomes impassable. Alas, I am expected home before November. In these remaining days before my departure, may I call upon you, Miss Talbot?"

Georgette welcomed winter's approach. "We are unlikely to meet again. My family will return to England as soon as my father has completed his business here. We long to see home. Are you native to New York, sir?" She bit her lip, but the question had already escaped. She hoped he would not misconstrue her curiosity as personal interest.

"My mother was born in the Hudson River Valley."

She smiled cautiously at the nonanswer and tried to imagine this virile Mephistopheles ever having a mother. "Your name is French. You must be descended from the Normans. My mother loves everything about France—except the government. I was tutored in Paris, but since I have the face of a pug dog, nothing succeeded in making me fashionable."

"Lapdogs are *de rigueur* in Paris, I hear." His voice quivered. Was he amused? She dared not meet his eyes to see.

"I once owned a spaniel, but my father refuses to buy me another."

"You prized this dog?"

"I adore animals," she said, eyes narrowing.

"I meant no offense, Miss Talbot. I, too, esteem dumb beasts."

The dance concluded, and he escorted her from the floor. "May I call upon you before I leave town, Miss Talbot?"

Georgette avoided his gaze. "Perhaps." She curtsied.

Someone bumped her from behind. Unbalanced, she pitched forward and bounced into Mr. LaTournay. The American's gloved hands gripped her bare shoulders and pulled her upright. Overpowering sensations whirled through her mind and body, and something pounded against her palms.

A man's embarrassed voice apologized. Georgette vaguely heard LaTournay give a sharp reply. Then his voice near her ear prompted another shiver. "Are you well, Miss Talbot?"

She felt his breath upon her face. Opening her eyes, she nodded. The hint of a smile curled his mustache. He released her shoulders to grip the hands pressed flat upon his chest—hands Georgette suddenly recognized as her own.

"Oh!" She snatched her hands from his grasp and pressed them to her cheeks. With a whirl of skirts, she hurried blindly away. At last, in the recesses of a drawing room, she paused to wipe tears from her cheeks. "What has come over me? Dear God, hide me from this evil!"

❧

"No, sir, the master is out, and I am ordered to tell you that Miss Talbot is ill with the headache and cannot receive callers," the butler, Montrose, said in a monotone.

"Give these to Miss Talbot along with my best wishes for her return to health."

Georgette listened from just inside the parlor door, clenching her teeth in guilt. That somber voice held unmistakable disappointment. When would the man give up? For five days in a row, he had attempted to see her.

As soon as the front door closed and Georgette heard Montrose pass the parlor on his way to the kitchen, she peeked around the door. After a late night out, her parents had not yet risen for the day, although it was nearly noon. Padding toward the stairs in her bare feet, she stopped short.

A bouquet of asters lay upon the entry table beside a plain calling card. "J. M. A. LaTournay," she read softly. Her fingers brushed the delicate blue petals. Such lovely flowers were difficult to abandon, but one of the maids would surely put them in water soon and carry them up to her "sickroom." For now, she had better return to bed before anyone suspected the truth.

❧

Late that night, Georgette snuggled into her featherbed, reading a novel by candlelight. Eyes wide, heart thumping, she sat up with a start when a knock came at her chamber door. "Who is there?" Then, recalling her role, she shoved the book under her blankets and lay back with one forearm across her eyes. "Enter."

The door opened and hesitant footsteps crossed the room to pause near her bed. "Miss?" It was Biddy, the elderly chambermaid.

"Yes?" She put a pathetic quaver in her voice.

Biddy whimpered like a puppy. How odd. Georgette lifted her arm slightly.

A puppy goggled down at her, kicked its dangling legs, and whined again.

Georgette's eyes opened wide, and she sat upright. Biddy

held the fawn-colored pug pup at arm's length. "The man told me to give it to you, missy. I am sorry to disturb you, but your parents are out, and Agnes hates dogs."

"Oh, he is adorable!" Georgette reached for the pup and clutched him close. The puppy's pink tongue washed her cheek. Laughing, she held him away from her face. "Where did you say he came from?"

"A man, missy. Just now, at the front door. A cloak concealed his face, but he left this card."

The puppy tugged at Georgette's braid while she read the inscription. "To Miss Georgette Talbot from a devoted admirer."

She flung the braid back over her shoulder. "Is he still here?"

"I doubt it, miss."

But even as Biddy spoke, Georgette scrambled out of bed, rushed to the window, and opened it wide. The street lamps below revealed a mounted horse standing in the middle of Broad Street.

"Hello!" She waved. The cloaked rider lifted his head.

"Missy! You'll catch your death standing at the window in your chemise. Your mother will be angry."

Biddy's outrage discouraged her not a whit. "Thank you," Georgette called down, cupping her hand around her mouth.

The rider lifted his hand. The horse wheeled and broke into a canter. Hoofbeats echoed down the empty city streets.

Georgette turned to meet Biddy's irate gaze, her hands clasped at her breast. "This is the most thrilling day of my life. Are you certain the man was a stranger, Biddy?"

The maid propped both hands on her scrawny hips. "You get back into that bed, missy, or I shall tell your mother about your showing yourself at the window in your chemise!"

"Oh, Biddy, do not be foolish. I am certain he saw only a billowing white object. What did his voice sound like? Did he seem young or old?" A dreadful suspicion struck. Might her admirer be Mr. LaTournay?

"He sounded foreignlike. Not English like you, but maybe French or Spanish."

An accent could be feigned. Georgette pulled on her bed-gown, watching the pup waddle toward her across the tumbled counterpane, his curly tail wagging. No matter his origin, she loved her gift. When he reached her, she scooped him up and kissed his velvety head. "I must take my puppy to the garden, then find him something to eat. What is your name, pup? You are entirely sweet."

two

For what fellowship hath righteousness with unrighteousness? and what communion hath light with darkness?
2 Corinthians 6:14

April 1775

For two hours Georgette sat and listened to a stand-in for the regular minister drone about the evils of disobedience to Mother England. Occasionally he referred to a Bible passage. Georgette tried to focus on the sermon, but her eyes kept straying toward a visitors' box across the church. The man seated there seemed familiar, though she could not see him clearly.

She was certain he had been watching the Talbot box. Perhaps he knew her father. She hoped he was not one of her father's gambling friends come to ask for payment. Papa never spoke of financial matters, but Georgette knew the situation at home was rapidly worsening. Montrose and two footmen had been let go over the winter, leaving only Biddy, Agnes, and Cook to keep the household running. For a family of high standing, two maids and one flighty Italian cook were insufficient household staff.

A disturbance outside sent a stir through the congregation. People glanced around, giving hushed exclamations of dismay. *Crack! Pop! Bang!* Cheering filled the streets, and the hoofbeats of running horses clattered along Broadway, yet the good reverend made no sign that he heard. Georgette decided the man must be deaf.

Several men slipped out of their boxes and headed for the

door, among them the tall visitor. Georgette felt as though the minister would never stop, but eventually he wrapped up his oratory with a prolonged benediction.

Members of the congregation questioned each other in hushed tones, hurrying for the exits. Georgette followed her father into the churchyard as her mother stopped to chat with a friend. Firecrackers popped in the middle of the street. Boys in ragged clothes shouted. Although she was curious about the cause of this clamor, Georgette knew she could not barge into her father's conversation with a group of men. She glanced about in search of Marianne.

"Good day, Miss Talbot."

Lifting one hand to shade her eyes from the spring sun's glare, she looked up. Her eyes widened, and heat rushed to her cheeks.

The visiting gentleman was Mr. LaTournay. "It is good to see you looking well," he said quietly. "I trust you passed a healthy and profitable winter?"

She avoided meeting his gaze. "I–I am well, Mr. LaTournay. You are back in town?" Too late she realized the absurdity of her question.

"For a time. Have you heard the news?"

"No. What has happened?" Eager for information, she looked into his eyes.

"Four days ago, American and British troops fought a battle at Concord and Lexington, two villages not far from Boston. A courier brought the news just minutes ago. It was a defeat for the British, by his account."

"Oh!" She covered her mouth with one hand and extended the other as if to ward off disaster. "How dreadful! What will become of us? Papa must agree to return to England now."

LaTournay grasped her outflung hand. "I hope not too quickly."

She yanked it away and glared at him. "It cannot be soon enough for me."

The flicker in his eyes told her that her shaft had struck home; still he persisted. "May I call upon you sometime this week?"

Her fingers seemed to burn where his had touched them. "I–I shall be busy."

"Mr. LaTournay! How delightful to see you!" Her mother arrived amid a rustle of petticoats and ribbons. Georgette wanted to groan.

"I hope you plan to call on us again soon," she said, dimpling and nodding. "As you can see, Georgette is now quite well and able to receive callers."

LaTournay's shrewd glance brushed Georgette. "Thank you for the invitation, Mrs. Talbot. Ladies." Touching his tricornered hat, he bowed and walked away.

Georgette exhaled slowly and closed her eyes. *Dear Lord, please let him never return!*

❧

"When next he calls, you will receive him." Her father's voice held the ring of steel. He paced the sitting room, hands clasped behind his back. "Biddy tells me LaTournay attempted to call upon you last fall and you turned him away." He jabbed a finger at Georgette. "Never again will you feign illness to avoid him. Attempt it, and I shall drag you downstairs in your shift to entertain the man!"

Georgette felt her facial muscles twitch as she fought back panic. "Papa, surely you would not force me to marry. I dislike Mr. LaTournay. He is evil."

Her father swore, grasped her arm, and jerked her forward. Eyes narrowing, he hissed through clenched teeth. "LaTournay is a leading citizen in this province. His past is none of your concern. You will encourage his suit in every way possible. Do you understand?"

Georgette tightened her lips. Her father tightened his grip. "Oww! Yes. I shall receive him."

He let go. Georgette rubbed her arm as tears spilled down

her cheeks. "But I shall never marry that man!"

Smack! The back of his hand against her cheek jerked her head to one side. He pointed a finger in her face. "Never speak so to me again! You will do as I say, and that is final."

Georgette fingered the welt left by his signet ring and felt her heart break.

❧

That evening several men arrived to visit with her father. Her mother retired to her chambers, leaving Georgette to her own devices. Shouts and occasional bursts of laughter from the parlor drifted up the staircase.

More gambling. Georgette flopped upon the bed. If her heart sank any lower, it would punch a hole through the bottom of Manhattan. With a wry smile, she visualized the entire island upending and sinking into the river.

Her little dog, Caramel, strolled across the bedclothes. "You sleep too much," she informed him, sliding his floppy ears between her finger and thumb. "But I adore you anyway. You mend my wounded spirits better than any physic." For weeks after Caramel's mysterious arrival, she had questioned her acquaintances about pug dogs. Did anyone have a dog with puppies? Had anyone recently sold a pup? Her investigation turned up no clues.

"I wish you could tell me about the man who brought you, Caramel. Did you like him? Is he kind to fat puppies? Or was the cloaked rider a courier for my real benefactor?"

Caramel snorted and leaped off the bed in search of a toy.

Hearing the crackle of fireworks, Georgette hurried to the window to watch them flame across the sky. A woman's hearty laugh rose from the street below, along with the clop of hooves on cobblestones. The tavern at the corner did brisk business. Lively band music drifted on the chill night air, and the glow of bonfires dotted the city. A sudden breeze held the promise of spring, the sting of sea salt, and a whiff of gunpowder and smoke.

Georgette inhaled deeply. Excitement flooded her veins. She craved adventure, thrills—and romance. Anything to escape the future her father planned for her.

"Lord Jesus? Are You listening to me?" Her recent decision to devote her life to God's service had provided little respite from boredom, and instead of miraculously disappearing, her problems had multiplied.

Caramel brought her a leather ball. Georgette tossed it. She heard his paws scrabble on the floor, and a thump indicated when the pug slid into the wall. Small wonder his face was flat.

"I do not understand Your refusal to answer my prayers, God. Papa plans to marry me to a reprobate, and Mummy smiles and tells me not to worry."

She accepted the slimy ball and threw it again. "Why would You put this desire for romance into my heart, then threaten me with a husband like Mr. LaTournay? I know I am to love You first, and I do. But I also wish for a loving husband and children. If You care at all, please send the right man to me soon. If only the admirer who sent my dog would make himself known." A long sigh closed her petition.

Rising, she rang for a maid to help her prepare for bed.

No response came to her summons or her prayers. Annoyed, she shut Caramel into her bedchamber and padded down the back stairs to the kitchen. Biddy and Agnes bustled to prepare refreshments for her father's guests. "Where is Cook?" Georgette asked as Biddy passed her, carrying a loaded tray.

Agnes gave her a glance. "Gone to join the celebrations, miss. Biddy and me, we hold little store by such goings-on, and the missus promised us extra pay to stay the evening. Too bad you have no young man to show you a good time tonight. 'Twould be unsafe for a lady alone. Every man in town will be out and about." Her gap-toothed smile was meant to be kind.

Until that moment Georgette had not considered sneaking

out, but Agnes's comment stirred her imagination. Who would know? She considered asking Agnes to sneak out with her but decided against it. The practical servant would go straight to Georgette's parents with her plans.

Other women managed to traverse the streets of New York unescorted. She was a strong, healthy girl. Why not? Surely the Lord would protect her from harm.

In her father's wardrobe, she found a woolen cloak. The guests' coachmen would see her if she used the front door, so she slipped into the garden and through the gate.

Eager and breathless, Georgette hurried her steps along Broad Street. Hearing footsteps behind, she turned but saw only a carriage passing on a crossroad. A shiver trickled down her spine, and she increased her pace.

There would be safety in numbers. Noise and glowing light from the direction of the common drew her on.

Sure enough, bonfires and fireworks illuminated a boisterous gathering on the green. A man stood on a podium delivering an address about the bright future of New York, frequently interrupted by cheers and whistles. The crowd surrounding Georgette consisted mainly of the lower classes, judging by attire and vocabulary. Yet she saw some well-dressed men and a few women in gowns finer than hers. Liquor flowed freely, and more than one interruption of the speech came from an overly enthusiastic drunk. The crowd laughed at such interludes and continued carousing. Some of the women exhibited themselves in ways no lady would approve, yet their gentlemen associates appeared to relish the display.

Are there no men left in the world who appreciate a woman of virtue? Or must a woman be vulgar to excite a man's genuine interest? Among the other young women, she had heard talk of men who lived double lives. Such men would wed none but ladies of quality, yet they took pleasure in the company of actresses and dancers, even fathering illegitimate children. Men like Mr. LaTournay, who preferred other men's wives.

If I marry, I want my husband to be satisfied with me alone. Most of these women are no more beautiful than I am. I could be as exciting to a man as they if I tried. She imagined embracing any of the rough men standing near the fire and grimaced. Many of them had not bathed in months, judging by the grime around their necks. Some appeared young and strong; a few wore fringed buckskin breeches and jackets; some were bearded and hulking. Perhaps she was too choosy.

One brawny fellow noticed Georgette. "What have we here? Are you alone, sugarcakes? This is my lucky day." He lurched forward and gripped her arm.

Georgette's yearning for romance took a plunge. She turned to escape, but the man twisted her arm and pulled her back. "Why so modest?" His filthy hand gripped her chin, and rancid breath filled her nostrils. "Give us a kiss."

Suddenly the fellow gave a yelp and fell away from her, his hands grasping at a black cord around his throat. As his back struck the ground, a hand gripped Georgette's shoulder, turned her about, and propelled her forward. "The lady, she is with me, monsieur," a heavily accented voice said in clear warning. Turning back, Georgette saw in profile a black-cloaked figure standing with feet braced, brandishing a driving whip.

The big man staggered to his feet, bellowed once, and charged like a bull. His challenger stepped aside and rapped him on the skull with the butt of the whip. He sprawled on the grass and lay there, moaning. His drunken companions laughed.

The victor replaced the whip in a waiting carriage. A voluminous hood concealed his entire head, giving him the appearance of the Grim Reaper.

Georgette turned to run, but the man's arm slipped around her waist. He pulled her away from the bonfire toward the dark streets. Squealing, she beat both fists against his forearm. "Let me go. You are no better than he to accost a lady so!"

"You need not fear; I intend you no harm," the Frenchman

said, setting her on her feet in the shelter of a large tree. "Do you not know what manner of business is conducted on the 'holy grounds' just beyond the common? Crazed, I think the lady must be, to wander alone in the wicked city, and more so on this night when men's blood runs hot."

Georgette shook her head in confusion. "Business? Do you mean the church?"

His laugh lacked humor. *"Innocente."*

Understanding dawned. Georgette's entire body burned with shame. "Are you saying those women are. . . ? That man thought I was. . . ? That you—no, never!" Horrified, she struggled to escape.

Her captor restrained her. "No, never!" he mocked in falsetto. But then his voice deepened. "And yet perhaps mademoiselle craves romance."

Gooseflesh prickled Georgette's arms. She sought a glimpse of the man's face but caught only an occasional glitter in his eyes, the reflection of a street lamp. "If–if I yearned for romance, it would be with a gentleman, not a ruffian. You Frenchmen are infamous for perfidy and. . .and passion."

When he chuckled, she regretted her suggestive choice of words. His grip on her upper arms seemed effortless, yet she was powerless to escape it.

Lifting her chin, she tried to sound confident. "Do you know who I am? My father will have you flogged if harm comes to me."

"Should harm come to you tonight, I would deserve such penalty, *ma fille.*" With one fluid motion, he again wrapped his arm about her waist and hauled her close. Her hooped skirts ballooned behind her. Although she held herself rigid and put up both hands to prevent her body from contacting his, Georgette made no vocal protest beyond a gasp.

"Regardez-moi, s'il vous plaît, ma belle fille."

She recognized enough French to know he had called her beautiful. "Let me go." She pushed at his chest. Her elbow bumped what proved to be a large pistol shoved into his belt. Whip. Gun. What other weapons did he wield? Might he be a soldier? Not with that accent. A French-Canadian trapper perhaps, come to the city for excitement and liquor.

His waistcoat felt soft beneath her hands, pleasant to touch. Or was it a shirt? Puzzled, she slid her hands over the thin fabric. Fringe. He wore buckskin. She heard the man suck in a breath, and a flurry of French followed, none of which she understood. He trapped her hands in an iron grip.

"So free with the touching you are. And you would return the favor?" His thumb traced her jawline.

She flinched in pain as he touched her cheek. "What are you doing?"

With a soft exclamation, he turned her toward the street lamp. Georgette blinked, cringing when he hovered too near.

"Eh, what has happened to your face?" His caress circled the welt on her cheek. "Did that dog strike you? I should have killed him."

"No—he did not do it." She recalled her father's cruel blow, and her breath caught, sounding much like a sob.

"Then who?"

Georgette felt her lips move, but no sound emerged. Feeling lost, she reached both hands to his chest as if to push him away. His thudding heart against her palms seemed familiar. His breath brushed her face—no hint of alcohol or tobacco there. What manner of man was this?

He released her and backed away. *"Mille pardons."* The hooded head bowed. "Such liberties are not mine to take."

Trembling, she searched for something intelligent to say. "Who are you?"

He caught her by the hand, turned, and began to walk along the street toward her parents' rented town house. "Promise you will never again venture into the city alone at night."

Regret pricked her conscience. "I was foolish to behave thus. I *am* a lady. You must believe me!"

Once more he exclaimed something indecipherable in French, and he slowed his pace. "I doubt not your purity of heart."

"What may I call you? I am Georgette Talbot."

"I know." His voice was quiet. "Did you like the dog?"

"The dog? Caramel! You gave him to me? But why? Who are you? Where have we met?" All too soon she recognized the brick town houses and storefronts of Broad Street. Had her parents noticed her absence?

"I first saw you dip your feet in the river and swing on a tree branch until I feared you would drop into the water."

"You saw me?" Georgette whispered. Like a child she had played that summer day, for once free of adult supervision. Or so she had thought. "The day my hat blew away."

"Your hair, it catches the sun and captures my heart. Your dog, he will remind, each time you look at him, that your devoted slave worships the earth beneath your feet. *Nuit et jour,* I dream of you."

"Oh–h–h–h!" Georgette's feet seemed to float well above the paving stones.

He stopped at the garden gate and released her hand. "Carriages still wait out front. You might yet slip inside unnoted."

"You are leaving? Will you not come inside? I wish to see your face."

He backed away. She caught the edge of his cloak. "Will I meet you again?"

"Assuredly, yes."

"When?"

"Ma petite Georgette." His features remained shrouded in darkness. "So desperate you seem. *Pourquoi?*"

"My father gave me the welt on my cheek because I refuse to marry an evil man."

"Your father seeks an evil man to marry his daughter? Pray, tell why." Satire laced his voice.

"He has already chosen one, although I am uncertain the evil man is yet aware of my father's plan. Papa has extensive gaming debts, you see. He did not gamble when we lived in England; it is the influence of this wicked city. I suspect Papa might—" She fell silent rather than reveal suppositions that put her father in an even worse light.

"And who is this evil man?"

"You must know of him, a Mr. LaTournay."

"I know the name. In what way is this man evil?"

Angered by his mocking tone, she snapped, "He pursues the wives of other men."

"You know this as fact?" His tone was equally sharp.

"His reputation is foul. My mother advises me to overlook such behavior in a man, but I cannot."

"Nor should you," he said. "A philandering man makes a poor husband."

The adamant statement warmed her heart, obliterating his former irony from her memory. "Are you married?"

"Not as yet, but when I wed, my heart will belong to my wife alone for as long as I live."

Releasing her hold on his cloak, Georgette covered her mouth with one hand.

He stepped forward and gently pulled her concealing hand away. She felt his breath upon her face, then the quick pressure of his fingers upon hers. "*Bonsoir* and *adieu*, Georgette," he whispered and strode away into the night.

three

But the LORD *said unto Samuel, Look not on his countenance,*
or on the height of his stature; because I have refused him:
for the LORD *seeth not as man seeth;*
for man looketh on the outward appearance,
but the LORD *looketh on the heart.*
1 SAMUEL 16:7

The hired carriage stopped before a mansion on the outskirts of town. Lifting her skirts, Georgette followed her parents up the broad front steps. A fine mist fell, and the entire world seemed gray.

"Everyone of importance in the province will be here tonight," her mother predicted. "Remember to smile and be genteel, Georgette."

"Yes, Mum." Georgette's interest in social events had waned.

After handing their wraps to waiting servants, Georgette and her mother hurried to the ladies' chambers to repair damages to gown or coiffure. When they returned, they joined her father in the queue of guests and shook hands with their hosts, retired Colonel Weatherby and his wife.

"Is it true this Whig pretense of a congress threatens to outlaw dancing and parties?"

"How dare they attempt to force such bans upon the law-abiding public?"

Snatches of disturbing conversation reached Georgette's ears as she picked her way through the crowds and joined a fluttering bouquet of young ladies near the refreshment tables.

Marianne waved her fan. "Gigi! Over here."

"Marianne, how are you?" Georgette slid into an open place against the wall.

"Well enough. You look lovely!"

"This is a remake of one of my mother's old gowns, and it is too small for me. Mother had Agnes tighten my stays until I feel ill." Georgette covered her mouth with her fan. "Alas, I am complaining again. I shall never learn to be content, Marianne. How do you do it?"

Marianne smiled. "Give yourself time to grow in God's grace, Gigi. You are a newborn babe in Christ; you cannot expect perfection from yourself."

Georgette sighed and pursed her lips. "My parents wish to hear nothing about my faith in Jesus Christ. They tell me I have been a Christian since I was baptized as an infant."

"That is what they were raised to believe. Just keep speaking the truth in a loving, respectful way, Gigi. Your interest in the Bible might inspire them to search for answers, too."

"People must acknowledge questions before they see a need for answers," Georgette said. "And it is difficult to point out fallacies in my parents' beliefs without sounding disrespectful. Had I not always been such a difficult child, they might be more willing to listen to me now."

Marianne patted her friend's arm. "You cannot change the past, Gigi, but the changes God has made in you since Christmastide, no one can ignore."

Guilt swamped Georgette. "You would not think so if you knew what I did last Sunday night." The secret of her escapade seared her conscience. "I can scarcely believe it myself." She longed to tell Marianne, yet a crowded ballroom hardly seemed the proper setting for a confession.

"No matter what you do, I shall always love and admire you, Gigi."

Georgette gripped Marianne's small fingers. "You are my first real friend aside from my sister. Most women are spiteful and insincere, but you? Never."

"You are good for me, as well," Marianne said.

A tall figure loomed over them. "Good evening, ladies."

"Mr. LaTournay, how nice to see you back in the city! A good evening to you." Marianne extended her hand in greeting. He bowed over it, then turned his gaze upon Georgette.

"I trust each of you ladies will honor me with a dance this evening."

Georgette couldn't force herself to smile, but she managed to acknowledge his greeting with a nod before realizing he would interpret the movement as an agreement to dance. While she struggled to think of an excuse, one of Mrs. Weatherby's daughters settled at the piano and played the introduction to a reel.

"I should be honored, Mr. LaTournay," Marianne answered after a brief silence. He took her hand and led her to line up with several other couples at one end of the crowded room.

LaTournay's claret-colored coat fit his shoulders perfectly. Georgette looked away, determined to find nothing admirable in the man. Dainty Marianne seemed a child beside that lanky scarecrow of a man, she decided.

Two figures blocked her view. "Georgette, this is Mr. Lester Pringle." Her father indicated a smiling young man. "I hear from reliable sources that he is a fair dancer."

Georgette stammered through a "Pleased to meet you." Her father moved on, leaving Georgette alone with the attractive young man.

"If we hurry, we may join this dance. Will you?"

She nodded. He led her to the dance floor and bowed as the music began.

"I understand you are come to New York from England a year ago. If that is so, you have already endured one summer's killing heat," he said as she rotated around him.

"And who spoke of me to you?"

Light sparkled in his eyes. "My friend LaTournay. It seems you have made a fair impression upon his sensibilities. He does not usually come to town early in the year, yet here we find him in April."

Georgette's smile faded. "I have no wish to impress Mr. LaTournay."

Mr. Pringle's brows lifted as he displayed healthy teeth in a grin. "Better and better."

"Do you like dogs?" She tried to imagine Pringle cloaked in the dark.

He laughed. "Once I was presented with a harrier pup, but I gave it away. Dogs are bothersome creatures—especially lap dogs. Utterly useless. Horses are my passion. LaTournay rides a brown mare I would give my eyeteeth to own. Have you seen her?"

"No."

He proceeded to wax eloquent on the finer points of this unknown horse. Georgette concentrated on her dance steps. The small floor seemed crowded with couples, and she noticed a stitch developing in her side. Mr. Pringle danced with more enthusiasm than grace.

"I see LaTournay observing us with something less than approbation in his mien," he confided against her ear, pulling her so close that their bodies nearly touched. "Shall we make him burn with jealousy? Do you long for my kiss as I long for yours?"

"No." Georgette jerked away in confusion. Again Mr. Pringle laughed aloud, causing stares of disapproval from nearby matrons. Georgette wished he had kept his mind on horses.

The ladies and men changed partners for a moment, and Georgette found herself curtsying to Mr. LaTournay. He took her hand. The room seemed uncomfortably warm. She was relieved to switch back to Pringle despite his impertinent behavior. For the duration of the dance, Georgette had trouble focusing on her partner due to her constant awareness of Marianne's partner.

When the dance ended, Pringle excused himself. Georgette caught the roguish twinkle in his eye as his hand brushed the length of her bare arm. Fanning her warm face, she settled upon a vacant chair. Another touch on her arm made her jump.

"Gigi, I saw you with Mr. Pringle. Does he dance like a dream?" Marianne's bright eyes begged for information.

"Mr. Pringle? He is pleasant enough, though forward. He laughs too loudly." Georgette flicked her fan. "Did you enjoy dancing with Mr. LaTournay?"

"He was polite, although I think he would prefer you as a partner, Gigi. He asked many questions. I told him about your puppy, Caramel, about how you like to read novels, and I even told him about your accepting Jesus as your Savior last Christmastide. I hope you do not mind."

Georgette sprang up. "My side aches. Would you care to stroll through the garden with me?"

Marianne laughed. "It is pouring rain out there, you goose! I may be warm, but I am not afire. I should think you would want to stay here where Mr. Pringle can ask you for another dance. At present, he is talking with Mr. LaTournay. I think his face expresses real depth of character." Marianne looked dreamy-eyed. Perhaps her personality held a touch of romance after all.

Pringle turned, caught them watching him, and approached, smiling. "LaTournay tells me you are to dance the next with him, Miss Talbot. Since this is the case, I would be delighted to meet your friend." He turned his gleaming smile upon Marianne.

Georgette made the proper introductions, and Mr. Pringle requested Marianne's next dance. "If you are available," he added.

Color flooded the girl's face. "Yes, Mr. Pringle," Marianne said. "I have no engagement."

He bowed, winked at Georgette, and walked away. Stunned,

the two girls exchanged looks. "Gigi, this is my fondest dream come true! Does my hair look well?" Marianne fanned herself until her curls flew about her face.

So I am to dance the next with Mr. LaTournay, am I? Georgette brooded. *I shall show him.*

The pianist concluded a minuet. Dancers left the floor, and Mr. Pringle arrived to claim Marianne. Georgette saw him trail a finger down Marianne's arm, bring her gloved hand to his chest, and look deeply into her eyes. Georgette shook her head. The man was far too confident of his own allure. Nothing like her mysterious rescuer.

"Miss Talbot."

That stilted voice lifted the hair on the back of her neck. Mr. LaTournay offered his arm, and Georgette accepted it. In his presence, all thought of defying his wishes vanished. "Remarkable weather we are having," she blurted.

"So it must be, since you have remarked upon it."

She swallowed hard and tried again. "Do you always come to town when the ships arrive from England?" She curtsied to begin the dance, thankful that her feet seemed to know the steps without her conscious direction.

"Usually. I also trade with the other colonies, of course. But, as you know, many items can be obtained only from your homeland."

"I wonder if Boston and Philadelphia are cities of culture and refinement. New York is rustic, in my opinion. We were surprised by the pigs that scavenge in the streets. I was told the beasts keep the streets cleaner, but I suspect my source spoke in jest. Pigs?" She winced. "Oh dear, do you raise pigs on your estate? Or was it sheep? I should think sheep would be cleaner beasts to have roaming the streets."

Her nervous chatter held his attention, and she thought one side of his mustache twitched. She now realized that the raised mark just below his left cheekbone was a reddish birthmark, not a mole. "No doubt you are correct," he replied, "but sheep prefer clean grass and fresh air to rubbish. I share their distaste for city life."

"I should think a man of your refinement would find country life dull." Unless he kept a collection of female admirers in the country as well.

"I have always before found town life dull, yet this spring I could scarcely wait to return. You have brought life to this dreary city, Miss Talbot. Perhaps someday I shall be privileged to show you the delights of rural living."

She would prefer to have his penetrating eyes focused elsewhere. Was it fear that raised gooseflesh on her arms each time he touched her hand? It must be!

"You have traveled nowhere in America outside this city?" he inquired as they traversed a circle.

"Not as yet. My mother often speaks of seeing Boston, but Papa says this is not the time for travel. One cannot tell whom to trust these days; there are so many traitorous colonists terrorizing honest subjects of the king. I would like to travel more. I did attend school in France for a year." They separated to dance with different partners for a moment, and she recalled telling him about her Paris schooling once before. He might find her company tedious and lose interest. All the better.

When the dance brought them together again, he spoke softly. *"C'est fort intéressant."*

Without attempting to translate, she answered lightly, "I confess that I understand little French. Although I attended school in France, I never claim to have learned anything there. Have you traveled?"

"I have never been to Europe."

Did he think her frivolous? For the first time, Georgette regretted her squandered opportunities. "New York is a British province. I mean, since you live here, you have been to England. Is that not true?"

"I am certain King George would find such sentiments

gratifying," he returned. When the dance ended, he bowed over her hand and kissed it, looking up at her with a quizzical challenge in his eyes. Georgette stared, openmouthed. Some extraordinary power emanated from the man. And those eyes. . .

"Miss Talbot," he purred, holding her gaze and squeezing her fingers. "You know, do you not?"

"I have no idea of what you are speaking!" Georgette snatched her hand away and unfurled her fan.

He straightened, eyes widening. Lifting his brows, he averted his gaze, and she saw his mustache twitch as if he fought a smile. "My mistake."

Georgette watched him walk across the room.

"Marianne, why is evil so alluring?" she demanded of her friend a few moments later.

The smaller girl allowed Georgette to maneuver her into an alcove. "Whatever prompts such a question, Gigi?"

Georgette's rapid fanning produced a gale. "That lord of the underworld. I want him to go away. I refuse to become one of his many conquests!"

"I thought you liked him. I tried to attract your attention while we danced just now, but you seemed absorbed in your partner."

"I hate him!" Georgette blotted out the memory of her fiery response to his slightest advance. "He uses other men's wives for his own enjoyment. He probably considers matrimony now only to add respectability to his family line."

Her other possible explanation was too humiliating to mention. Was she so undesirable that her father resorted to extortion to provide her with a husband?

"My father is acquainted with Mr. LaTournay," Marianne said. "He came to dine at our house the other night, and I found him pleasant company. He associates with the leaders of our province and is respected by most if not all of them. Gigi, the man has no need to improve his status by marrying well."

Georgette stifled a wave of jealousy. Mr. LaTournay dined with the Grenvilles? Had he transferred his interest to Marianne?

"I mean no offense," Marianne continued, "but if the truth be known, I would not have thought he would consider you at all, Gigi. Yet even Mr. Pringle remarked while we danced tonight that you and Mr. LaTournay thought yourselves alone in the room."

Georgette covered her hot cheeks with both hands. "No! Oh, Marianne, did you not tell me I should seek a godly man to marry? I am far too easily beguiled by worldly men." She attempted to draw a deep breath and nearly cried out at the sharp pain stabbing her side. Growing still, she waited for the discomfort to pass.

"You and I both know we may not be allowed to select our husbands. My parents will consider a man's religion before promising my hand, but I fear yours will not. You must be in prayer that God will guide their selection."

"I shall pray," Georgette agreed, nodding. "Have you seen my mother? I wish to go home. I can scarcely draw breath. Agnes laced me too tightly."

❧

Across the room, Pringle and LaTournay conferred. "You are correct: The blond in pink is a choice armful," Pringle observed. "Keep your eyes half-closed, and she is *très belle.* The little one also has appeal, though she is freckled. Her hair is like moonbeams."

"She is Howard Grenville's daughter."

Pringle brightened. "The Long Island merchant and land owner? Miss Grenville's appeal multiplies beyond the tally of her freckles. She is the more comely of the two, in truth. Miss Talbot's mouth makes me think of a frog wearing lip rouge."

"Her mouth is lovely," LaTournay snapped.

"Ah!" A slow smile curved Pringle's lips, and his blue eyes twinkled.

LaTournay folded his arms. "Leave Miss Talbot to me. She is not your type."

"She will soon bore you—she is no wit."

"She amuses me."

Pringle shrugged. "You have never before asked me to leave a woman alone. Will you dance with her again?"

"I hope to." LaTournay frowned. "Here comes Lady Forester."

"How can you sound morose? Delia Forester is a sensible recipient of your passions—safely married, husband away much of the time, and ever so willing!" Pringle elbowed LaTournay in the ribs. "Why the sudden loss of interest?"

"I would obtain a wife of my own." Leaving his friend to absorb this information, LaTournay stepped forward and bowed to Lady Forester.

"A wife!" Pringle's exclamation reached his ears.

❧

"Thank you for the dance, Miss Talbot." Mr. Pringle bowed. His blond hair gleamed in the candlelight, and mischief twinkled in his blue eyes. Georgette sat down as he turned to Marianne and asked, "Will you honor me once more?"

The girl fairly leaped to her feet. "Oh, yes!" She took his extended hand and let him lead her to the floor.

Georgette was thankful to be rid of the arrogant fellow. The tales he told of Mr. LaTournay's exploits with married women verified her worst fears. To make things worse, she could not draw breath without feeling as if a knife pierced her side. She should never have accepted Pringle's invitation to dance a reel.

She searched the room for her mother only to observe Mr. LaTournay talking with a dark-haired woman who laid a possessive hand upon his arm and gazed into his eyes with evident desire. How shameless! Jealousy scorched Georgette's heart. The one man who expressed interest in her just had to be the town lothario.

Turning her face away, she started around the perimeter of the crowded room. The pain increased with every step. To grip her rib cage and pant would be ill bred, but etiquette began to seem trivial compared to the agony in her torso. She was suffocating, possibly dying, and no one noticed. Finding a seat behind a potted tree, she toppled into it and wished for oblivion. She pressed one fist against her teeth and the other into her side. Tears burned her cheeks.

"Miss Talbot, allow me to help you."

"Please!" Her sanity reached out and clung to the quiet voice.

"Can you rise? Lean against my arm, and I shall take you to a drawing room where you can lie down."

The voice gave her courage. She nodded. The room swirled around her in waves of color, music, and conversation. Leaning heavily on her rescuer's arm, she concentrated on remaining conscious. They passed through a doorway, and the party's commotion receded. "We are nearly there," the man said just as Georgette's legs buckled. After a moment's scuffle with her recalcitrant hoops and yards of fabric, he lifted her in his arms. She peered up at a familiar bearded face.

Mr. LaTournay was as strong as he looked, and his musky cologne filled her senses. "My mother," she whimpered into his shoulder, feeling strangely secure.

"I shall bring her to you. Here we are." His shoulder shoved against a door. Carefully, he maneuvered Georgette's hoops through the doorway.

As awareness returned, panic rose. What did he intend to do with her? "It is dark in here!" She pushed weakly at his chest.

He stopped. "Can you stand while I light candles?"

Although she was not sure, she nodded. He lowered her feet to the floor, discreetly tugged the ruffles down to conceal her petticoats, then left her swaying in the doorway. Georgette closed her eyes and fought to remain upright. Soft light filled the room.

"Come, rest here, and I shall go in search of your mother."

Blindly, she reached for him and leaned into his strength, letting him guide her to a settee. Bending to lie down was agony. Once she lay flat, her grip on his coat lapel relaxed. He stepped back, and her hoop sprang up. Without looking, he dropped a large cushion atop the billowing fabric. It settled unsteadily on her legs.

Georgette wanted to die. He tucked a pillow behind her head. Feeling a soft handkerchief upon her tear-dampened cheek, she reached up to take it from him.

"Better?" He was a hovering shadow, composed and reassuring.

"Yes. I can breathe more easily now," she said. "Mum insists that my waist be as small as Juliette's, but I am fatter than my sister." As soon as the words escaped, she wished to take them back. Of all things, she did not wish to bring the man's attention to her figure.

"Perhaps it would be wise to loosen your stays."

Her eyes flew open and his face came into focus. No longer shadowy and comforting, he was again evil incarnate. She pressed both hands to her bosom. "My mother will help me!"

"Of course. I shall return directly." He backed away.

Had she misjudged him? No one could be entirely evil, after all. "Thank you, Mr. LaTournay," she said as he opened the door.

"It is my pleasure to serve you."

Her heart thudded against her concealing hands. When he was gone, the last of her composure disintegrated. It was too painful to sob, but more tears scalded her cheeks.

❧

"Whatever do you see in the wench? Her nose looks like a little blob, and her mouth is immense like a—"

"—a frog wearing lip rouge," LaTournay said in unison with Pringle. "She says she has the face of a pug dog." He swirled the coffee in his cup.

Pringle guffawed. "She even has the mournful brown eyes!" His brows lifted. "Tell you what—give her a bauble or two, entice her into the garden during the next dance, and take your fill of those smooth white shoulders. Then you can forget her and return to normal. What do you say?"

LaTournay leaned both elbows on the coffeehouse's marred tabletop and fingered the corners of a newspaper. "Why did you dance with her again?"

"You mean after you warned me off? You needn't look murderous. 'Twas all for you, my friend."

LaTournay said nothing.

Pringle spouted profanities, half laughing. " 'Tis the truth. Granted, I tried the garden tactic myself, but she complained of her side hurting. I left the field open for you to play the gallant rescuer—a part you bungled, if I read the ensuing scenes correctly. Whatever did you say to her?"

"Nothing untoward. I have only to approach, and she blanches as if I were a death's head."

"Hmm. No doubt your reputation precedes you. It is all over the city that you prefer to dally with married women. Everyone knows of your torrid affair with Delia Forester." His grin reached from ear to ear. "So I bent Miss Talbot's ear with a few embellished tales of your libidinous exploits. You should have seen her blush, you satyr!"

"Sincere appreciation for the character endorsement," LaTournay said. "No wonder she panicked when I attempted to help her."

"Women find rakish men exciting. Once she discovers your wealth, she will be eager clay in your hands."

"I find it difficult to believe that her father has failed to inform her of my financial standing."

Pringle flung his hands up in surrender. "Very well. I promise to keep hands off until you have tired of her. Satisfied? My sights are set on richer game—Grenville's daughter. My government job is not paying as well as I expected, so I might have to sacrifice pleasure for the present and take the matrimonial plunge."

"Your government job?"

Pringle glanced up and down the long table to make sure no one was listening. "A colonel in Boston—old friend of the family—asked me to check out the situation here in New York and carry messages."

"I see."

"It is infuriating what these Whigs do while the governor is gone, and they think they can get away with it." His expression turned serious. "I need solid information about plans and munitions, about who can be trusted to support us."

"I just arrived in town."

"What use are you?" Only half joking, Pringle sat back on the bench and drained his cup. "Tell me if you hear anything. The occupation and embargo of Boston have nearly destroyed the Pringle shipping business, and Whig associates are making it impossible for my father to recoup his losses. I am in worse straits than Talbot, since I have no daughter to sell off to a susceptible dupe. He would have to pay me to take her off his hands."

"Miss Talbot probably does not know how to spin, weave, or cook," LaTournay mused, "but she could learn."

Pringle shook his head. "The maid is passing fair, but I have seen far better. And if you think Talbot will let you wed her without first defrauding you of a considerable sum, you are a greater fool than even I realized."

"She is far from plain," LaTournay's voice rasped.

Pringle cleared his throat. "Worst thing is to get attached to a woman. Forget about her. Think of her as an angler—her charms are the lure, and she fishes for any rich man who will take the bait. You must be like the wise old trout: Steal the bait and avoid the hook. Oldest game in the world."

"Far from attempting to lure me, Miss Talbot would banish me if she had the power. She has depth, Pringle, a sagacity and sincerity one rarely encounters in a woman."

Pringle snorted and thumped a fist on the tabletop. "Same old story. Desire overrides reason. The deceitful woman will demand all and give nothing, and when you have given all, she will take it and run, leaving you with that barbed hook in your heart forevermore."

"So you prefer to play hunter rather than hunted. Unlucky Miss Marianne Grenville," LaTournay said.

"She is just a woman with a rich father. I shall give her a few babies to occupy her mind, then start enjoying life again. Who are you to criticize? At least Miss Grenville does not belong to another man."

The dregs of LaTournay's cup were bitter.

four

How long wilt thou forget me, O LORD? for ever?
how long wilt thou hide thy face from me?
PSALM 13:1

Hearing the bell ring, followed by voices in the front hallway, Georgette rushed from her room to peer over the edge of the dark stair landing. Mr. LaTournay handed his hat and cane to Biddy. Morning sunlight poured through a leaded window above the entry door, bathing him in a pool of brilliance.

A few locks of loose hair dangled around his cheekbones, giving him an unkempt appearance. By contrast, his brown wool coat fitted his rangy build perfectly, its simple lines displaying quality.

Snorting and woofing, Caramel descended the stairs in a wild rush. LaTournay bent to greet him. "Ah, the diligent watchdog," he said, rubbing Caramel's sides while the dog fawned about his boots. LaTournay looked up—Georgette had no time to hide. The corners of his dark eyes crinkled, and he lifted a hand in silent salute. She tried to smile back.

"Mr. Talbot will see you. This way, sir." Biddy showed him into the study. He ducked his head to enter.

"Has insanity taken over this entire city?" Georgette heard her father ask after the usual greetings. "It is no longer safe to walk the streets."

"I am certain this unrest will soon pass and the streets will be safe once more," Mr. LaTournay said.

"I pray you have come to me with an offer, LaTournay—"

The door closed, ending Georgette's eavesdropping. Hope and dread warred within her pounding heart. "Help me,

Lord." The feeble prayer was the best she could do.

❧

Sometime later, while Georgette sat on her window seat, gazing blankly at a book, her mother's call rang down the hallway. "Georgette? Come here, child." Georgette rose, shifting Caramel from her lap to the cushions. He snored on.

As she entered her mother's chambers, Georgette crossed paths with her beaming father. He patted her cheek and winked. "Good girl." Grateful for his rare approval, she smiled.

Her mother sat up against a silk-padded headboard, her abundant hair cascading over plump shoulders. A wrap supporting her chin tied in a knot above her forehead. Ribbons on her cap rustled as she nodded and smiled. "You look well this morning."

Her mother's mornings began and ended late.

"Thank you," Georgette said.

"It appears that, despite your unfortunate illness, your appearance the other night was adequate to attract a serious offer for your hand. So you see, the stays served their purpose. Your father and I could not be more delighted." Her blue eyes glowed. "Think of it! Your sister's husband comes of good family and has excellent prospects, but he lacks the wealth of your Mr. LaTournay."

"I care nothing for wealth. I would marry for love, Mother." Her chest felt tight. *He asked! He truly asked for my hand in marriage!*

Her mother babbled on. "Juliette must economize, but you? Never! I shall plan your trousseau immediately, for there is no time to waste. As you know, our finances have been somewhat strained of late, but your betrothed promises to pay for anything you need. How thrilling to have my daughter snare such a catch! Although I had suspected an attachment earlier, I knew for certain Saturday night. I told Victoria Grenville that he was enthralled with you, and now I am proven correct. He could scarcely take his eyes off you even as you danced with other men, and I do not believe he asked more than one or two other ladies to dance all evening. Of course, he might have done so after we were obliged to leave, but it matters not, for you are the lucky maiden he chose as his bride!"

Georgette barely heard her mother's ravings while her thoughts and heart waged war. Her logical mind found voice. "I cannot believe that you and Papa would sacrifice your daughter to an immoral man."

"What nonsense!" she said, swinging her legs over the side of the bed and flinging on her bedgown. "You will marry him and do it with becoming modesty."

"I would rather die."

An outright lie, and her mother knew it, for her lips curved. "You should run away to the stage, my dear. Perhaps your father is right and I have spoiled you. A dutiful daughter will yield to the greater understanding of her elders and marry the suitor they select for her."

"Loving parents would not select a suitor whose behavior the daughter finds disgusting." Georgette did not have to fake the break in her voice.

"Child, you speak of things outside your understanding. Mr. LaTournay is no better and no worse a man than any other. You cannot be immune to his melancholy eyes? And such legs and shoulders! Were I but ten years younger, I should contend for the fellow myself! If you care anything for the honor of the Talbot name, and I believe you do, you will obey as a dutiful daughter should. The wedding will take place as soon as decently possible, and that is the end of the matter."

❧

Georgette looked up from the book she was reading. Her mother stood in the doorway. "Your father is away, and I am leaving for the church, dearest girl. Unforeseen difficulty has arisen regarding your wedding. Dr. Inglis is being unreasonable about the entire affair because of Mr. LaTournay's

Catholic baptism, and I fear we shall have to convince another minister to perform the ceremony. One would think that in a progressive city like New York, a minister would not be so bound by tradition."

"He is Catholic?" Such a thing had never occurred to Georgette. Placing her book on the window seat, she rose, picked up Caramel, and strolled about the room. "If Dr. Inglis disapproves, should it not be taken as proof that this marriage is disapproved by God?"

Her mother shook her head. "Mr. LaTournay is a Christian, Georgette. I do not believe he is active in religion of any kind, so what should it matter to you? He has agreed that your children shall be baptized in the church of your choice."

Georgette decided she would prefer to know the worst. After placing Caramel on the floor, she confronted her mother directly. "Does Mr. LaTournay wish to marry me, or is Father forcing him into marriage using some threat?"

Her mother appeared insulted. "To say such a thing about your own father! Why must you disparage your charms, my child? Mr. LaTournay desires to marry you, and that is all you need to know."

Covering her mouth with one hand and holding her elbow with the other, Georgette shook her head. "The entire affair is distasteful, and I cannot comprehend why you and Papa seem pleased. Mr. LaTournay may plan to take over the Talbot estates or Papa's business."

"Stop hiding your mouth, speak clearly, and stand up straight. If you would cease questioning everyone's motives, life would be much happier for all of us." Without meeting her daughter's eye, she closed the door.

Biddy brought up a calling card moments later. "A lady to see you, missy."

Georgette read the name. "Lady Forester? Are you certain she wishes to see me?"

"She said your name clear enough, missy."

"I shall come down directly." Her thoughts spinning, Georgette checked her reflection in the mirror and hurried downstairs.

"She is in the parlor," Biddy whispered in passing. Squaring her shoulders, Georgette nodded at the wrinkled little woman.

Lady Forester turned as Georgette entered the room. Her bright green eyes blinked in evident surprise. "Miss Talbot?"

Georgette's heart gave a jolt of recognition. "Yes?"

At first glance, the woman was stunning—voluptuous figure, raven hair, those amazing eyes, and a low voice. Yet as light from the parlor windows touched the lady's face, Georgette saw that her skin was rough.

The hint of a sneer curled Lady Forester's mouth. "I cannot believe it. There must be more to the tale than I am aware."

"Madam?" Georgette began to suspect the woman's purpose, and anger heated her face.

"LaTournay must have some ulterior motive for choosing you as his bride. Perhaps he wishes to allay my husband's suspicions." She perused Georgette's figure.

"If you intend only to insult me, I must request you to leave." Georgette spoke through clenched teeth.

"I came in kindness to warn you. LaTournay may avow fidelity, but he will not keep that promise. Such a man can never satisfy his needs with one ordinary woman." Her tone implied that she, Lady Forester, transcended the common female.

The parlor door opened and Biddy announced, "Miss Grenville to see you, miss."

Georgette had never been more pleased to see Marianne's angelic face. "Madam, have you met Miss Grenville? Marianne, Lady Forester. She is just leaving."

Lady Forester's lips disappeared into a tight line. Angry red blotches marred her complexion. Lifting her skirts, she brushed past Georgette.

As the front door closed with a thud, Marianne looked

puzzled. "Did my arrival anger her, Gigi?"

"She was angry before she arrived," Georgette answered. "I am overjoyed to see you, dearest friend. You rescued me from a most unpleasant encounter. I thought the woman might rend me with her claws as well as her tongue."

Marianne's cheeks turned pink, and her eyes expressed sympathy. "She came concerning your betrothal to Mr. LaTournay. Word of the match has spread throughout town. I pray you are happy, Gigi."

"Come." Georgette linked her arm through Marianne's and led her into the garden. The girls strolled between beds of sprouting perennials. "What have you heard?" Georgette asked after a thoughtful silence.

"Only that the banns would soon be read for your engagement. Gigi, I have news of my own."

Grateful for the change of subject, Georgette brightened. "Tell all."

"Mr. Pringle has been calling upon me, and Papa has given permission for us to court. Yesterday Mr. Pringle took me riding into the country in his chaise. He tucked the lap robe around me and worried lest I take a chill. Imagine! The day was balmy." Marianne giggled. "His voice gives me the shivers, so sweet and mellow. Oh, Gigi, I have admired him for years. Never dared I believe that he might notice me!"

"I am happy for you."

"And are you happy?" Marianne's gentle blue eyes held concern.

"I shall never know happiness again unless God provides a way to escape this nightmare."

"Gigi, you mustn't say such things. God cares for our needs, and He wants to fulfill our desires, but sometimes we desire wrong things. We need to have our hearts in tune with His perfect will."

Georgette gave a sharp laugh. "My parents pledge me to a soulless rake, and I am to see this as God's will?"

Marianne cringed yet refused to yield. "I think you should start asking God to give you love for Mr. LaTournay. God can use a wife's godly example to bring her husband to Himself. Mama says she did not love Papa when she married him, but she prayed to love him, and now she cannot imagine life without him. They adore each other."

"But your father is a good man. If your mother did not love him, at least she did not despise him when they married. Do you know why that Forester woman came to see me? She told me that Mr. LaTournay will still be hers even after I marry him."

Marianne looked wise. "That is what she wants to believe. I know better. Mr. LaTournay adores you, Gigi. You have the advantage over Lady Forester, no matter what hurtful things she says. Your love will make him forget her entirely."

Tears burned Georgette's eyes as longing burned her soul. Turning away, she covered her face with both hands. "I confess—I wish that were true. But never will I be able to trust him. He travels to the city often, Marianne, and she will be here waiting for him. I do not want to share my husband with anyone. I cannot marry him. I simply cannot!"

Marianne wrapped her in a tender hug. "If you refuse even to try to love him, all hope of happiness is gone. How my heart aches for you, Gigi!"

Arms about each other's waists, the two girls circled the garden at a slow pace, heads bowed.

Georgette sighed. "Very well. I shall attempt praying to love him."

❧

Mr. LaTournay joined the Talbots for dinner that evening. Georgette picked at her food and kept her gaze lowered while the men talked politics. More than once her parents tried to draw her into the strained conversation. When these efforts produced no response, she sensed their perplexity escalating into irritation.

Mr. LaTournay's presence was like an ache in her soul. Sorrow blocked her throat.

"Tell us about your home, Mr. LaTournay," her mother demanded. "Do you have servants?"

"There are many people living on the farm. Our servants work for hire; we keep no slaves. All speak at least some English, and several have children. We also have frequent guests drop in at Haven Farm. My wife will not lack for company when I am away on business."

Georgette winced inwardly.

"Haven Farm," her mother repeated. "How charming. Did you name it?"

"My grandfather, Piers Vanderhaven, settled the land and chose its name."

"Did you grow up there?" Georgette's father spoke around a mouthful of food.

"My mother was born on the farm," Mr. LaTournay said. "My grandmother died when my mother was born, and Grandfather never remarried. He left Haven Farm to me and my sister, Francine."

"So your mother was Dutch?"

"My grandfather was Dutch, but my mother's mother was French, as was my father." He sounded uneasy.

Georgette sensed displeasure emanating from her parents.

"You seem so English," her mother said.

"Neither France nor Quebec claims my loyalty. New York is my home, and it receives my allegiance."

"As a colony of His Royal Majesty, George III," her father added.

Georgette sneaked a look at her fiancé across the table. He met her gaze as though he had been waiting for her notice. "I am deeply committed to country and family. My wife will have no cause for fear or complaint."

Despite a strong desire to roll her eyes, Georgette faked a smile and returned her attention to her filet of cod. Hearing a whimper, she noticed that Caramel was not in his usual begging spot beside her chair.

He sat beside Mr. LaTournay.

❧

Mr. LaTournay stayed for only a short time after the meal ended. Her parents retired to the parlor; Georgette could hear them arguing as she climbed the stairs. In her room, she bathed and prepared for bed, then lavished extra attention on Caramel, throwing a ball until even he tired of the game. The little dog scrambled up on the bed and flopped to his side, panting with lolling tongue. "At least Mr. LaTournay likes you, my precious puppy. Some men do not care for lap dogs." Circling the pug with her arms, she rested her forehead on his heaving side. "Why must he be so attractive, Caramel? I despise him, yet I crave his attention."

Biddy rapped at the door for the second time that day and held out a folded paper. "Sorry to disturb you, missy, but a man asked me to give this to you."

"A man?" Georgette hopped to her feet and broke the seal. "Did you recognize him?"

"I should say 'twas the same man what brought that dog, miss. He wore a cloak and spoke quiet-like, but I heard the foreign in his voice."

Georgette sucked in a deep breath as she read. "Biddy, do not tell a soul, but I am to meet him in the garden."

Biddy's watery eyes widened. "A rondyvoo, miss? I'll be quiet as the dead."

Not even the morbid simile could diminish Georgette's excitement. With Biddy's help, she dressed and hurried downstairs. Her father dozed over a book in his study. Georgette tiptoed past the door and rushed along the hallway.

Moonlight silvered the rose trellis and threw stark shadows on the stone walkway. Shivering, Georgette tightened her grip on her knitted shawl. Would he come? She peered through the wrought-iron gate, but no cloaked figure waited outside.

"Georgette."

With a startled cry, she spun around. A shadow detached itself from the deeper shadows near the wall. "Hello." Her voice quavered.

"You came."

"You thought I would not?"

"I know of your betrothal to Mr. LaTournay." He stepped closer, a looming specter. "You no longer believe him to be evil?"

She studied her own linked fingers. "I have no choice but to marry him."

"You have many choices, *petite grenouille*. Does he know of your father's coercion? What man would wish to marry a woman by force? Have you no affection in your heart for the poor wretch?" His voice held a caressing note.

"Lady Forester called upon me today." The words poured out before she thought them through.

A pause. "Indeed." Cracking ice sounded warm in comparison to his tone.

"She told me that Mr. LaTournay would not keep his marriage vows to me, that I could never satisfy him." Aghast, Georgette lifted her hand to her mouth. This was an unknown man, not a father confessor.

He turned with a swirl of his cloak and walked the length of the garden path, spun about, and returned. "Her words contain no truth. You heard the vengeance of a resentful woman, *bien-aimée*."

"And how would you know?"

"I know much about women and their devious ways. I also attest that any man of sense would be more than satisfied to have you as wife. LaTournay, for all his faults, is generally accepted as a sensible man."

"You are acquainted with him?"

"I am."

"You say 'any man of sense.' Does this mean that I appeal only to a man's brain?"

He murmured something in French. "You play with fire, *ma belle Georgette.*"

"Yes, I feel that fire within each time you speak my name." She pressed her hands over her heart. "I do not understand myself! Why is it that my heart responds to a man even while my mind doubts him? My mind knows Mr. LaTournay to be an immoral and ungodly man, yet my heart yearns within me when he is near. And you—I know so little of you, not even your name, and yet. . ."

"Pray do not leave me suspended thus." His long arm reached out, and his warm hand clasped hers. She wrapped her other hand around his.

"And yet you. . ." She struggled for words. "You seem like one to whom I may safely bare my soul."

His grasp tightened, and she heard him sigh. "Georgette, this charade must—"

"Marianne, my friend, tells me that I must pray not only for Mr. LaTournay's salvation from sin, but also that God will teach me to love him. You and I must never again meet alone, kind benefactor, for I am pledged to another. From this time on, my loyalty and love must belong to Mr. LaTournay alone."

His hooded head bowed low, and silence stretched between them. Rousing, he lifted her hand, turned it, and touched his forehead to her wrist. "I am your slave and your footstool. Be merciful, I adjure you, *belle grenouille.*"

Before she recovered her equilibrium, he disappeared into the shadows once more.

five

If ye then, being evil, know how to give good gifts unto your children, how much more shall your Father which is in heaven give good things to them that ask him?
MATTHEW 7:11

Georgette dutifully prayed to love Mr. LaTournay. Although her fiancé's moral code still disturbed her, she began to appreciate the possible benefits of marriage to such an intelligent man. As spring passed into summer, listening in on LaTournay's conversations with her father stimulated Georgette's thoughts and broadened her understanding of the turbulent political conflicts engulfing the city of New York.

She depended upon her betrothed for protection from an uncertain future. Not only did he always possess the latest news about the fluctuation of power between Whigs and Loyalists, he also seemed undaunted by it. More than once, Georgette heard her father quote Mr. LaTournay's remarks or advice to associates, citing the younger man as a reliable authority.

One rainy afternoon, Georgette spread the Thursday edition of the *Gazetteer* on the library floor, scanning it for conversational material that might impress her fiancé. Most of the news centered on politics. Everything in life seemed to revolve around politics, since the Provincial Congress now prohibited most social activities. The possibility of war was no longer whispered behind hands in drawing rooms. Now it was shouted in the streets—insults to Mother England, threats to her loyal subjects.

Although the Talbots showed carefree faces to the world,

Georgette observed her father's tension in his constant smoking and recognized her mother's fear in her strident tones. For the first time, Georgette saw her parents as frail beings seeking security in every possible place—except the one place they might find it. Her attempts to discuss God and the meaning of life with her mother met with sighs and rolling eyes of rejection. The one time Georgette spoke in her father's presence of seeing God's guiding hand in their present circumstances, she feared he might do her physical violence.

Would life be different with Mr. LaTournay? Despite Marianne's assurances that a godly wife might influence her husband to seek the Lord, Georgette knew such change was unlikely. Not that Mr. LaTournay was unkind—but then, he was not yet her husband. A man would reveal only his best side before the wedding. Georgette's probable fate would be a marriage of mutual toleration, as exemplified by her parents.

Mr. LaTournay spent much of his time away from the city, never offering explanation for his absence. Georgette had not seen him for more than a week. She feared he might be visiting Lady Forester, although the latest gossip, according to her mother, testified that the two had parted ways. Georgette did not have the nerve to ask if he had other female friends. If he did, she thought she would rather not know. But then again, she did want to know.

Of all things, she feared unrequited love. The torture of loving a man who cared for other women! Already Georgette suffered. If he never loved her in return, she would want to die.

Scowling, she attempted to concentrate on the news. Utterly ridiculous, how her thoughts could wander from war to love. As if the topics connected. No reasonable woman expected love in her marriage anyway. To become an interesting companion to Mr. LaTournay, able to support her end of a conversation—now that was a sensible goal. Hence the newspaper.

But Georgette's thoughts and gaze soon wandered off the page again. *"When I wed, my heart will belong to my wife alone for as long as I live."* The memory of that beautifully accented voice echoed in her dreams night and day.

Since the night she sent her mysterious visitor away, she had heard nothing from him. Although he spoke no overt words of love—at least, not in English—Georgette nevertheless knew that he cared for her. Would she ever see him again? Pressing her wrist to her lips, she recalled the warmth of his touch.

She flopped back on the rug, wrapped both arms over her head, propped her bare feet on the seat of a chair, and studied the ceiling's plaster moldings.

Her wedding day. One hand resting on Mr. LaTournay's arm, she emerged from a huge gothic cathedral. Her face like marble, cool and lovely, she bore her fate with dignified forbearance. Suddenly a giant black stallion pounded into the churchyard and reared. Its rider's cape flowed from magnificent shoulders as he leaped to the ground, drew a sword, and challenged Mr. LaTournay to a duel.

Mr. LaTournay, tall and deadly, posed with saber in hand, his shirtsleeves billowing. Swords clashed. Women screamed and fainted.

With blood staining his white shirtfront, Mr. LaTournay slowly fell to his knees, reaching one hand to her. There in the churchyard, for the first and last time, she held her husband in her arms and kissed him. After weeping for the love that could never be, she rode away with her romantic hero. . . .

But Mr. LaTournay could not die. Even in imagination Georgette could not bear the thought of him suffering injury. Yet unless her husband died, it would be evil to leave him for another man.

She decided the cloaked hero should be wounded instead,

and the confrontation must take place before, not after, the wedding ceremony.

Reeling from a gash in his side, her hero tossed her behind him on the saddle and galloped away. Clutching his broad shoulders, she begged him to stop and let her bind his wound. He slid to the ground, and she cradled him in her arms. Tenderly, eagerly, she reached for the concealing hood—

The library door creaked. "I am so pleased you came by. We were beginning to wonder what had become of you. I have many questions. Georgette, are you in here? She was here a moment ago. I cannot imagine where she has disap—Georgette?" Her mother gasped at the sight of Georgette scrambling to her feet.

Mr. LaTournay stood at her mother's side.

Georgette brushed her skirts, feeling guilty heat pour into her face. She had not bothered to don a hoop and stays that morning, and the pink-flowered gown was one of her oldest. Her hair must be a sight after her gyrations on the rug. "I was. . .I was reading this week's *Gazetteer.* Good day, sir."

He bowed. "Good day, Miss Talbot. Do not apologize, madam; your daughter had no warning of my arrival. It is not to be expected that she would sit in readiness at all hours. Today's news must make interesting reading. Did you learn of our governor's return?"

Although his manner remained stilted, his tone was kind. Georgette felt short of breath, knowing how ridiculous had been her imaginings. "I had not heard of it."

"I asked Biddy to bring us tea in the parlor," her mother said. "Please join us, Georgette." In a whispered aside, she added, "And fix your hair!"

When Georgette entered the parlor a few minutes later, the conversation broke off and Mr. LaTournay rose to seat her at the tiny table. Smoothing her skirts, she smiled in his direction as he settled into the chair across from her mother. Caramel plopped between Georgette's skirts and Mr. LaTournay's boots. Her father remained in his favorite chair across the room.

Georgette's mother lifted the teapot. "It is growing difficult to find tea. I fear our cook purchased this on the black market. Do you take cream and sugar, sir?"

"Both, thank you." Mr. LaTournay handled the fragile teacup with practiced ease. His tanned hands were clean, even to the fingernails. He seemed cool and neat, as always. Georgette never needed to pardon an unpleasant odor while in his presence. Even his teeth were nearly perfect. She studied his mouth as he conversed with her father.

Her parents faded away.

Mr. LaTournay and she, a married couple, drank tea together in a shadowy room. Noticing that her husband needed more cream, she rose to serve him and dropped a tender kiss upon his cheek before returning to her seat.

Or would she kiss the top of his head? Or his lips? Could any woman ever feel comfortable enough with this man to display affection freely? How would he react? Bearing in mind his reputation, she knew he could not be as cold and impervious as he seemed.

He dabbed his mustache with a napkin.

Georgette's mother cleared her throat.

Realizing she had been staring, Georgette took a sip of tea and burned her lip. Her mother glowered. Mr. LaTournay's expression remained neutral, although he appeared somewhat flushed.

Could he read her thoughts? Oh, the curse of an unbridled imagination!

"So Governor Tryon is returning? I have always wished to meet him," Georgette blurted. "I have seen the warship *Asia* lying at anchor off Governor's Island. Now I shall watch for the governor's ship."

"He is to return, and therein lies the city's dilemma," Mr. LaTournay said. "The new commander in chief of the American armies, George Washington, is scheduled to arrive in the city on the very day of Tryon's return. Both men will expect a parade and official welcome, yet it would be unfeasible to hold two parades at once. Only Broadway is large and straight enough to accommodate a parade."

"Hmph. Who cares about the illicit general of an illegal army?" her mother said.

"From all I hear, Washington is a man to command both respect and admiration," Mr. LaTournay said quietly. "I have a wish to see the most talked-of man in America."

"Yet he is not to stay in town more than a day," Georgette's father added from his armchair. "Governor Tryon, the king's official, is vastly more important. Surely the city will show him the welcome he deserves after more than a year's absence. Some thought he would never return at all."

"All will be well now that Governor Tryon is back," her mother said. "I hope he demands the return of the British soldiers to Fort George and disarms the dangerous rabble who have ruled the streets these many weeks."

"I should like to see a parade," Georgette said.

"Then I shall take you," Mr. LaTournay offered. "Both men are scheduled to arrive in midafternoon, but perhaps that will change. We shall walk, so wear sturdy shoes." He placed his empty teacup in its saucer and again blotted his mustache. "Thank you for the tea. Miss Talbot, I wish to speak with you of plans for the future. Will you walk with me in the garden?"

"I need to confer with you afterward, LaTournay," her father said in a languid yet pointed manner. "There are details yet to be settled."

Georgette's mother gave her a warning look. Nodding to assure her good behavior, Georgette rose, brushed crumbs from her skirts, and led the way outside into a gray and gloomy afternoon. The garden, dotted with rain puddles, seemed smaller than ever before. Caramel sniffed and snorted his way along the wall, pausing to dig beneath a flowering shrub.

Mr. LaTournay paced a short track between two planters. His stride reminded her of. . . She shook her head to dislodge the traitorous memory.

"The minister of the Methodist church has agreed to marry us," Georgette said quickly to conceal her overwrought nerves. "My mother prefers early September. I hope that will suit you. It must be a small ceremony, but we shall have a reception here afterwards."

He paused before speaking. "I am aware of your parents' plans, but I do not wish you to feel rushed into marriage. Take the time you need to fully prepare, both emotionally and physically. I must warn you that we live simply at Haven Farm. Your everyday attire will consist of woolens and strong boots. It would be best to travel north before winter sets in, but if you cannot prepare in time, I shall return for you at whatever date you choose."

"I am willing to comply with the current arrangements." She attained a tone of self-sacrificing humility. "The banns have been published, and the wedding date was announced in the *Gazetteer*. Besides, I already own a quantity of serviceable clothing."

Another pause. "If you are certain."

She turned away. "I would not wish to inconvenience you."

"You misunderstand my meaning." He grasped her shoulder. She shivered, barely restraining herself from ducking away. He turned her to him and lifted her chin, but she refused to look up. "Miss Talbot, you need never fear me. Your welfare is my foremost consideration."

Georgette nodded.

A long moment passed, and she heard him exhale. "If you

please," he said in a whisper, "may I kiss you?"

Conflicting thoughts whirled in Georgette's head, disappearing into a void. Again she nodded, then closed her eyes. Warmth touched her lips, living, tender. Her lips parted, and he kissed her again. His strong arms slipped around her waist, pulling her close to his chest. She heard and felt his rapid breathing, tasted tea in his kiss. She craved more of these wondrous sensations, but the embrace ended abruptly. Georgette opened her eyes to meet his gaze. He removed her arms from around his neck and took a step back.

"Perhaps waiting would be foolish after all."

Georgette felt his thumbs stroke her wrists. "What?" Helpless to comprehend her own desires, she jerked her hands free and covered her burning lips, shaking her head.

Shame propelled her away and sent her stumbling into the house. She heard him call, but the numbness of her heart prevented any response.

❧

Georgette scarcely noticed Caramel's snoring. Eyes wide, she lay upon her bed. Dried tears made her face itch. Evening sunlight painted golden windowpane reflections upon the slanted ceiling of her bedchamber. A rain-freshened breeze stirred the window curtains. She could hear gulls mewing as they wheeled over the rooftops, and light traffic rattled along Broad Street. The Bible lying open upon her chest rose and fell with her uneven breathing.

Someone rapped at her door. "Missy?"

"Come in, Biddy."

The wooden door creaked open. "I have a note for you, missy, from Mr. LaTournay."

"Is he still here?" Georgette closed her Bible and sat up. She reached for the folded pyramid of paper. Beside her, Caramel stretched and yawned with a squeaky sound.

"He's been talking with Mr. Talbot in the study. Mr. LaTournay looks sad, missy," the maid dared to comment.

Georgette unfolded the paper. Caramel shoved his nose in the way as if to read it first. She pushed him aside and studied the elegant script.

> *I humbly beg your pardon and await your convenience in the garden.*
>
> *L*

"Thank you, Biddy."

"You wish to send him a note?"

"No, I shall come down."

Georgette watched until the door closed behind Biddy. If she were to refuse Mr. LaTournay's summons, her father would demand an explanation.

Rising, she splashed her face with water from the basin on her dressing table. Her eyes felt gritty and probably looked swollen. She trembled at the thought of speaking to Mr. LaTournay, and the knot in her chest forced out yet another sob. Georgette cupped her mouth with one hand, then touched her lips, recalling his kisses.

Did Mr. LaTournay's kisses affect Mrs. Forester the way they affected her? The thought of that woman in his arms twisted like a knife into Georgette's heart. Once again, she prayed for release—either from her fears or from this betrothal.

She had recognized passion in his eyes—those unfathomable eyes that could scorch and chill in the same glance. Although being desired by a man thrilled her, Georgette knew it was not enough. Mr. LaTournay had desired many women, by all accounts, yet his passion never endured beyond a month or two.

"Dear God, spare me the pain of becoming the latest in his string of discarded lovers. Help me to love him no matter what." Her face crumpled, but she swallowed the sob. "Oh, how blessed I would feel if You were to cause him to love me as I love him!" Caramel led the way downstairs and waited for Georgette to open the garden door. He dashed over to greet Mr. LaTournay and grinned while having his sides thumped. Georgette heard Mr. LaTournay speak to the dog, though his voice was too low for her to discern his words.

He straightened to his full height as she stepped outside. His gaze seemed to pierce her.

She hoped her eyes were no longer red.

"Miss Talbot, can you find it in your heart to forgive my behavior?"

Had his behavior been worse than hers?

She nodded shortly. "Even as God for Christ's sake has forgiven me."

"Ah." The response held elements of both admiration and amusement.

A wave of courage and resolve lifted Georgette. "Are you a Christian?"

"I was raised in the church."

"Do you believe that salvation comes through faith in Christ?"

He blinked. "I do."

"Will you study the Scriptures with me? I have a need to understand more about God, yet much that I read is beyond my comprehension. If we were to study together, perhaps I could profit through your superior understanding."

She read surprise and interest in his expression. "I am honored by your request," he said.

A certain hitch in his pronunciation caught her ear. Georgette found the apparent speech impediment endearing, though it seemed unfair that even the man's flaws attracted her.

" 'Twill seem strange to greet you on the morrow without revealing all that has passed between us," she said, taking a step closer to him.

Shadows darkened much of the garden, though the sky overhead still shone bright blue. Mr. LaTournay's bare head caught sunlight reflected from a window. His hair and beard reminded Georgette of a beaver pelt she saw once, thick and glossy brown.

He stepped forward. "I must be away but shall see you Sunday at church."

"And for the parade; do not forget your promise." She reached out one hand.

Georgette saw one of his brows twitch in response to her unskilled flirtation. Taking her hand, he bowed slightly. "I shall not forget."

His touch recalled vivid sensations. "Good evening, sir." Once again, Georgette pulled away and fled.

six

A sound of battle is in the land,
and of great destruction.
JEREMIAH 50:22

LaTournay's gaze wandered across the sanctuary of Trinity Church until it rested upon Georgette in the Talbot family box. Although she appeared to listen to the sermon, he saw vacancy in her stare. Her mind must be far away. As if sensing his regard, she glanced his way. Her face grew rosy as her gaze fell from his. What did she read in his eyes to make her blush and look away? Blinking, he settled into his seat and pondered the matter.

Dr. Inglis read Psalm 147. LaTournay could not recall hearing this passage before, but then he was not as familiar with the Bible as he should be. Today the words caught at his heart. Opening the Bible he had purchased the day before for the purpose of serious study, he located the Scripture and followed along.

"He telleth the number of the stars; he calleth them all by their names. Great is our Lord, and of great power: his understanding is infinite. The LORD lifteth up the meek: he casteth the wicked down to the ground. . . . He delighteth not in the strength of the horse: he taketh not pleasure in the legs of a man. The LORD taketh pleasure in them that fear him, in those that hope in his mercy. . . ."

LaTournay tried to picture God, infinite and almighty, caring for the needs of His creation. A being so powerful would remain unimpressed by the fastest of horses, the strongest of men, the greatest of battles. The one thing that brought Him pleasure, according to the psalm, was a man who feared Him and hoped in His mercy.

Although he acknowledged God's existence and supremacy, LaTournay had always assumed the Creator remained detached from His creation. Yet this psalm suggested that God desired a more personal relationship with people. With him.

Les Pringle, beside him in the visitors' box, snored. LaTournay elbowed him. Pringle turned another snort into a cough. "Thanks," he whispered from the side of his mouth.

When the service ended and the congregation filed outside, Pringle hurried to intercept Georgette and Miss Marianne Grenville. He slipped between the two young women, tucking an arm around each. "Lovely ladies, I am the luckiest man alive. To think that today I shall accompany the two of you to the welcoming parade for our governor!"

The spurt of anger caused by the sight of another man's hand on Georgette's trim waist startled LaTournay. He hesitated to approach the group, uncertain of his welcome.

"I believe Mr. LaTournay has other plans for today." Georgette stepped out of Pringle's reach. Her lips curled in annoyance. Sunlight filtered through her straw bonnet, dotting her face.

She glanced up, met LaTournay's gaze, and blushed. Her fair skin frequently betrayed the strength of her emotions, though he found it difficult to determine their course. Did this blush reveal pleasure or pain?

He watched as she stiffened her backbone and faced him. "I am pleased to see you here today, sir, although the sermon left much to be desired." She extended one gloved hand. He bowed over it.

"Gigi, you must not say such things!" Miss Grenville said. "People will hear."

Beside her, Pringle grinned and lifted a brow at LaTournay.

"Church is for sermons about God, not about politics," Georgette said, reclaiming her hand.

"I appreciated the Scripture reading," LaTournay said.

Miss Grenville's frown vanished. "That is wonderful. A good day to you, Mr. LaTournay." She was a pretty woman, slender and blond. He understood Pringle's interest.

"Good day to you, Miss Grenville. What is this name by which you address Miss Talbot?"

"I call her Gigi, for the two letter G's in her name," she answered, beaming at Georgette. She tucked one hand into the crook of Pringle's elbow. "I imagine we shall see you at the parade today."

After Pringle and Miss Grenville strolled away, Georgette made an obvious effort to be friendly and natural. "At what time shall we commence our walk?" She fingered her bonnet strings, pushed her gloves into place, and shifted her Bible from one arm to the other.

"I shall come for you at two o'clock. My landlady has promised to pack us a luncheon basket. If you prefer, I can hire a chaise, since it will be a long walk."

"The day is warm but not unpleasant. I shall enjoy walking with you." She lifted her sparkling brown eyes as high as his chin, then dropped her gaze to his boot toes. "My parents are pleased that we shall spend the day together."

"As am I, Miss Talbot."

She sucked in a quick breath and released it in a little burst. "Two o'clock then. I shall be ready." Giving a wave, she hurried to follow her parents from the churchyard.

Lucille and Frederick Talbot made a handsome couple—Frederick dark and dignified, Lucille blond and shapely. In LaTournay's estimation, Georgette exhibited the finest qualities of both parents. He had not realized the Talbots walked to church. Frederick probably could no longer afford to hire a coach.

He watched the family promenade along the street until Georgette's bobbing skirts disappeared around the corner. He headed for his boardinghouse.

"LaTournay, wait!" Running footsteps sounded from behind him.

Panting and grinning, Pringle caught him by the shoulder. "I have scarcely spoken to you these three weeks. What have you been doing? I seldom see you anymore."

"Business often takes me out of town. Politics are the ruination of profit."

Pringle gave a sharp laugh. "That I know. I assumed you were also wooing. I heard of your betrothal to the Talbot wench." He shook his head. "I still say you are crazy. The woman's head is a vacuum. Granted, she has the form of a goddess, but so does Lady—"

"Your pursuit of Miss Grenville's fortune prospers?"

Pringle winced. "It goes well enough, but I begin to have regrets. Though I am an unabashed scoundrel, I begin to think Miss Grenville is an earthly angel. She talks constantly about God. To appease her, I profess interest in such things, but my acting ability strains when it comes to praying and confessing sins and such."

"Because you have no sins to confess?"

Pringle chuckled at the jibe. "Sometimes I wonder if she loves me only because I present a challenge. I have an ambitious goal: Before this day ends, I shall coax a kiss from that saintly maid, and she will enjoy it. I hope the governor is late and doesn't come ashore until well after dark. He is scheduled to arrive at four o'clock, you know."

"Colonel Lasher has a militia company waiting at Coenties slip, where Governor Tryon is expected to land. Another company travels with four members of the Provincial Congress to Newark, where they hope to meet General Washington and detour him to the Hoboken Ferry," LaTournay said.

A burst of profanity indicated Pringle's loathing of the militia. "As far from Coenties slip as possible, eh? Trust New York to butter both sides of the bread. And where will the rest of Lasher's companies be?"

"At a halfway point, ready to greet whichever personage arrives first. Absurd, but necessary."

Pringle scowled. "Nonsense. No reason in the world to make a fuss over this Virginian upstart who dares take arms against England. I cannot help wondering what Parliament is thinking to let this rebellion linger on. Why do the *Asia* and the *Kingfisher* not send a few firebombs into the town and make them think twice about entertaining the enemy?"

"Either ship could burn New York to the ground, but what would such aggression accomplish? A ruined port is of no use to England, and violence against these rebels seems to harden their resolve."

"Have you been asked to take an oath of loyalty to this provincial travesty they call a congress? I shall resist to my dying day. I may not be an upstanding subject, but my loyalty belongs to the king." Pringle's eyes flashed indignation.

"Beware how loudly you speak, my friend. I, too, have scant use for the Sons of Liberty, as they call themselves. Yet several members of the Provincial Congress are loyal British citizens who desire a peaceful resolution to this conflict. Their complaints against England are not without basis." LaTournay paused at the door of his boardinghouse and faced Pringle. "Enjoy your day with Miss Grenville. She seems a worthy young woman, and I would not like to see my fiancée's friend hurt."

"Point acknowledged. Perhaps we shall see you about town." With a roguish grin, Pringle sauntered on, swinging his walking stick.

❧

At five minutes past two, Georgette sat waiting upon the front stairway, rolling her parasol between nervous fingers. The gauze tucked about her shoulders itched and tickled her neck. Sweat beaded on her forehead until she patted it away with a hankie.

Caramel brought his leather ball, dropped it at her feet, and backed off with a hopeful woof. Georgette obliged him by throwing it down the hall.

A knock came at the door. Caramel abandoned the ball chase and reversed course to thump his front paws on the front door and bark. When Georgette opened the door, the pug danced about Mr. LaTournay's feet and yammered. She raised her voice above the din. "Please come in. We no longer have a butler, and the maids are off this afternoon."

He obediently entered the hall and set down a laden basket. Caramel pushed his flat nose beneath the cloth, his curly tail wagging. Mr. LaTournay went down on one knee and pulled the dog away. "No, that isn't for you, unless you plan to come along on our walk. Then I might be convinced to share." Caramel rolled to his back and let his tongue loll from one side of his grinning mouth. After pulling off his gloves, Mr. LaTournay rubbed the dog's chest.

Georgette lifted Caramel's leash off its wall hook and paused to watch the man play with her dog. His gentleness surprised her.

What would he think of the way Georgette had acquired the pug? Would he be resentful of her secret beau? More important, would he have just cause for jealousy?

He glanced up. "Is anything amiss?"

"Why, no, not a thing." Except for her nerves. "Do you not think the day is too warm for him to join us? Caramel loves a walk, but his legs are short."

"I shall carry him if he grows tired." He took the braided cord from her and looped it through Caramel's collar.

"Very well. I am ready for our outing. Is this gown suitable?" The green-sprigged white linen was among her most becoming frocks. Georgette settled her straw bonnet over her curls and tied its ribbons beneath her chin.

"You are springtime itself," he said. "I shall be the proudest man in town." Lifting the basket with his left hand, he handed her the end of Caramel's leash and offered her his right arm. "Shall we?"

"Indeed, we shall," she said, slipping her hand into the crook of his elbow. She could hold both dog leash and parasol with her other hand. "My parents are entertaining guests for luncheon. They plan to attend the parade for Governor Tryon."

"I had thought we might join the crowd greeting Washington. I am acquainted with the governor, but this Virginian general will be a new face. Two other generals will arrive with him—Philip Schuyler and Charles Lee." He escorted her through the front door and closed it behind them. "Schuyler is an important man in the northern parts of this colony."

Georgette reclaimed Mr. LaTournay's arm and fell into step beside him as they headed north on Broad Street. When Caramel lunged toward a tree, her parasol whacked the top of her bonnet. Tugging the dog back to her side, she continued the discussion. "I cannot understand how these men who fought so bravely for our country during the war against the French and Indians could now turn traitor and fight against England."

"It is a different war and a different cause. Such men would not shift their loyalties lightly, you may be sure. Perhaps we should listen to speeches today and learn what we may about their reasoning."

"Would that not be treasonous?" She searched his stern profile for reassurance.

He pressed his lips together and gazed over her head across the rooftops. His eyes, she noticed, were a muddy brown in hue. Yet they were arresting eyes, with their thick dark brows and lashes.

"Do you wish to take a side in any controversy simply because of tradition and blind loyalty?" he asked. "Or would you prefer to understand the motives governing the actions taken by both factions, then choose the position most tenable in regard to your beliefs and convictions?"

Startled by the question, Georgette scrambled for an honest answer. "I would wish always to do what is right in the sight of God," she said.

"Exactly as I believed you would answer." He sounded pleased.

"But how could God be pleased by treachery? Is it not true that God puts kings in power? Our king is head of the Church of England. Dr. Inglis preaches that rebellion against the king is rebellion against God." Engrossed in the conversation, Georgette paid no attention to her surroundings. Her troubled gaze still searched LaTournay's face, and she clutched his arm like a lifeline.

"I understand the appeal of this argument to you." He patted her hand and slowed his pace. "Tyrants have used it throughout history to retain power. Although it is true that God raises and topples kings and kingdoms, it is also true that not all those He allows to rule are good and upright. If I understand correctly, Christ, not any human king, is head of the church. When a king abuses power and oppresses his subjects, it behooves those subjects to protest such injustice."

Georgette considered his words. "What if the king will not listen?"

"There you have put into words the vital question that has been debated up and down the coast of this continent these many years past. A similar situation long ago brought about the Magna Carta and the beginnings of republican government."

"I have often heard you discuss politics with my father. Always you spoke of taxes and representation, but this is the first time I understand the reason why so many colonists have joined the rebellion. Not that it is important for me, a woman, to understand such things, but—"

"*Au contraire!* You must realize what is at stake." Right there in the street he stopped, looked down into her eyes, and spoke earnestly. "I want you to know, and I want you to think, pray, and consider. As my wife, you will be affected by every decision I make."

His defense of the Whigs sounded entirely too sympathetic

to Georgette. Yet, transfixed by his stare, she could only nod, unable to voice her questions. Relaxing, Mr. LaTournay pulled her hand back into place upon his arm and continued their stroll. Caramel trotted beside Georgette's whisking skirts, his head and tail high.

"I do not intend to frighten you," Mr. LaTournay continued, "but you must be aware of the uncertain times in which we live. Look at the militia companies gathered here upon the common. Raw boys, most of them. Do they look ready to fight His Majesty's troops? And yet the Massachusetts militia, largely comprised of old men, farmers, and young boys, has fought admirably more than once these past months."

Georgette studied the uniformed troops drilling on the village green. Might her hero be among them? One of them, a handsome fellow, caught her eye and smiled, losing the beat of the march. The man behind him gave him a rough shove. Her heart thudding, Georgette turned away and attempted to portray scorn. "And these are the people this General Washington plans to lead against our British troops? How can he hope to win?"

Mr. LaTournay merely shook his head. Together they walked past the unsavory section of town, turned west on Read's Street to Greenwich Road, and headed north along the riverbank. Carriages passed them on the road, and other couples and family groups meandered along the highway north. The crowds increased as they approached the ferry landing. Caramel no longer tugged at his leash, and his tail had lost its jaunty curl.

"Are you hungry yet?" Mr. LaTournay asked. "This might be our best opportunity to partake from this increasingly heavy basket."

Georgette laughed. "You ought to have spoken sooner."

"There are shady places here along the river. See? Others had the same idea." He indicated a family of five seated on a blanket near the shore.

"A lovely big tree stands at the top of that knoll, away from the road. May we dine there with a view of the river?" she suggested. At his nod, she hoisted her skirts and led the way.

Mr. LaTournay spread the blanket and waited while Georgette fluffed her skirts into a circle. "I shall set out the luncheon, if you like," she offered, reaching for the basket. Caramel flopped down on the grass to pant.

As soon as Mr. LaTournay was seated, she handed him a lamb pasty wrapped in cloth. "Will you ask a blessing on our food?"

He nodded and bowed his head. Belatedly, he removed his hat. Holding it to his chest, he spoke slowly. "Almighty God, You have provided this food for us. It amazes me that You would notice us humans, yet You say we are important to You. I ask that You will lead Georgette and me in Your ways. Teach us to fear You and to hope in Your mercy. Amen."

He slid his hat back upon his head and bit into the pasty. Georgette wondered at the contradictions of his character. How could a man of such ill repute pray so convincingly?

They ate in silence for several minutes, watching the pedestrians and carriages, squinting in the sparkle of sunlight off the Hudson River. Georgette wanted to learn more about Mr. LaTournay, yet she did not know how to begin questioning him. He seemed a private person, as if a high wall protected his inner emotions. The brief glimpses she'd had into his heart left her wary.

Why did she feel as if she knew her covert admirer more fully than she understood her overt fiancé? The question always remained: Why would such a man choose Georgette Talbot for a wife?

Caramel recovered when the aroma of lamb reached his twitching nose. Sitting up and pawing the air, he begged for pasty. Mr. LaTournay rewarded his antics with bits of meat, then took him down to the river for a drink.

When they returned, Georgette offered Mr. LaTournay

the remaining strawberries. "I fear I have few skills that will be helpful on a farm. I cannot cook or milk a cow, and my sewing skills are merely adequate."

Settling back on the blanket, Mr. LaTournay lifted a brow, no doubt surprised by her abrupt comment. "My sister can teach any household skills you wish to learn." He popped a berry into his mouth.

"Your sister lives on the farm?"

"Francine helps run the farm and estate." His long fingers fondled Caramel's ears.

"She is unmarried?"

"Francine recently married Jan Voorhees, our foreman; they live nearby on the property. She is my elder by two years. Before leaving home in spring, I told her of my intent to marry. She will be pleased to have a sister. The main house will be ours alone, shared only with the servants. I hope to travel less often after we are married."

Georgette determined to make their home so pleasant he would never wish to leave.

❧

When General Washington and his retinue arrived, an enthusiastic crowd greeted them. To Georgette's surprise, a member of the New York Provincial Congress introduced Mr. LaTournay to the officers. Mr. LaTournay was one of few men present tall enough to look General Washington in the eye while gripping his hand. The two men seemed to take each other's measure, and Georgette recognized reserved approval on both sides. Mr. LaTournay was invited to join the group of dignitaries for a short reception at the nearby home of Lester Lispenard, a local brewer, but he graciously declined.

While the New York crowd waited for the parade to begin, Georgette and Mr. LaTournay wandered off a short distance and found a shady tree. Mr. LaTournay again shook out the picnic quilt and laid it upon the grass. Georgette flopped down too quickly to be graceful, dropped her parasol, and leaned her back against the tree trunk. Caramel watched the proceedings from his makeshift bed inside the empty picnic basket. He was a solid little dog, but Mr. LaTournay did not seem to mind carrying him.

"My father often speaks of your connections and influence, yet I remained ignorant of your true importance to this colony," Georgette said. Mr. LaTournay's apparent support for these traitors puzzled her.

"The importance of any farmer or merchant lies mainly in the commerce he undertakes. Do you mind if I remove my coat?"

Observing the sweat trickling down his face into his beard, she took pity. "No, sir." She would have liked to remove her shoes. Mr. LaTournay laid his coat on the quilt and ran a finger beneath his cravat. "You may remove that also if you wish," Georgette said.

He whipped off the tie and opened his shirt at the neck. "Much better." He lay back on the quilt, folding his hands behind his head and crossing his ankles.

Georgette tried not to notice the wet patches on his waistcoat and shirt—or the flat expanse of his stomach. "I do not understand whether New York remains faithful to England or intends to join the rebellion."

He squinted at the sky through his lashes. "I wish I could tell you what New York will do, but I cannot read the future. God alone knows what will come."

More questions swirled through Georgette's mind, but she could not find words or courage to phrase them. Caramel snored in the basket. A louder snore informed her that Mr. LaTournay slept. Georgette leaned over to examine him. A pulse beat in his throat, revealed by his open collar. Her hands ached to touch him.

The flood of passion his proximity stirred had become familiar to Georgette, but this new camaraderie she felt for him took her by surprise. Could a husband be a friend? She enjoyed talking with him, being with him—and not always with romance in view.

Politics never concerned her in the past, yet recently she found the subject intriguing, no doubt due to Mr. LaTournay's influence. He seemed to hold himself aloof, as a dispassionate observer above the fray of political affairs.

Georgette felt confidence in his leadership. Although, now that she thought of it, she had no clear idea in which direction he intended to lead. Of course, Mr. LaTournay would never participate in treasonous acts. Of that much she felt certain. Perhaps his intent today was to become aware of the enemy's strengths and weaknesses through observation.

Noticing something, she peered closer. On the shaved skin at one side of his neck, what appeared to be a scar ran diagonally toward his chin, disappearing into the thick beard. The skin around it was slightly puckered. How had he acquired such a wound? Georgette would have liked to part his beard and see how far the scar extended. The thought of him sustaining painful injury caused her to frown.

Had they not been within easy sight of dozens of people, she might have been tempted to kiss him. How would he react? Her imaginings brought a wave of heat to her face.

Folding her arms over her middle, Georgette lay back against the tree and closed her eyes. The next thing she knew, a warm hand cupped her cheek. "Wake up, Georgette. The parade is about to begin."

She stirred and sat up abruptly. "What time is it?"

"An hour has passed while we dozed. Several additional militia companies have arrived." Mr. LaTournay was already wearing his coat and cravat, looking almost as neat and composed as ever. Caramel rambled about amid nearby shrubs, sniffing fascinating scents.

Georgette was still blinking sleepily when Mr. LaTournay took her hands and pulled her to her feet. She helped him fold the quilt and stash it into the basket. "Ready?" he asked as soon as she had settled her parasol over one shoulder. He plopped Caramel into the basket atop the quilt, and this time, instead of offering his arm, he reached out a hand. Despite her sweaty palms, Georgette clasped his hand and followed him back to the Lispenard mansion.

When they arrived, the parade was forming ranks. Mr. LaTournay gave Georgette a running commentary as it passed them. After the militia companies came the New York dignitaries, followed by the three Continental generals and their staffs. An honorary escort of Philadelphia's light horse came next, and the noisy crowd of New Yorkers fell in behind. Georgette found herself cheering for General Washington and the proud men in uniform, although she could not have told why. Perhaps the quiet dignity of Washington influenced her emotions—he was an awe-inspiring figure upon his prancing horse. And Mr. LaTournay seemed to respect him.

They followed the parade south along the riverbank into town, back to the common, and down Broadway. More people gathered to cheer as the parade passed. Georgette gripped Mr. LaTournay's hand, waving her folded parasol in the air. "I shall be quite hoarse and sunburned by the end of the day," she confessed laughingly. "The governor, whenever he arrives, will receive no cheering from me, I sadly fear."

The day was still warm, although evening approached. Long shadows of trees and buildings striped the road. Disheveled, sweaty, and happy, Georgette shouted to make herself heard. "This is like a holiday!"

Mr. LaTournay squeezed her hand and smiled. Pressed by people on all sides, Georgette nevertheless felt an emotional connection with him as though they were alone. The crowds provided opportunity to jostle against him without appearing obviously brazen.

"LaTournay!" A man elbowed his way through the throngs, waving and hollering. "What are you doing in this mélange?"

seven

The L*ORD* *lifteth up the meek:*
he casteth the wicked down to the ground.
PSALM 147:6

Les Pringle gripped Mr. LaTournay and Georgette each by the shoulder and halted them in the middle of the boulevard. "Miss Grenville is waiting just over there. She spotted Miss Talbot's parasol, though I didn't believe her at first. Come out of this farcical parade and join us! The governor delayed his arrival out of pure politeness; he lands at eight o'clock. We've plenty of time to get over to the slip and greet him."

People bumped Georgette in passing, and one man shouted for them to stop blocking the way. Still, she was surprised when Mr. LaTournay followed Mr. Pringle's orders and shepherded her to the east side of the road.

Marianne greeted her with a hug. "Gigi! We looked for you two all over town and began to think you decided not to come. You're wearing your green sprig—I adore that gown!" She greeted Mr. LaTournay, saw the dog in his basket and wrinkled her nose in distaste, but made no comment. "What happened to you two? However did you get caught up in that pandemonium? We saw those uniformed men posing as officers. Is it not disgraceful? Mr. Pringle and I decided they are all decidedly gauche—especially the gaunt fellow with the pack of dogs following his horse."

"That would be General Charles Lee, late of His Majesty's army," Mr. LaTournay said.

Mr. Pringle spat on the ground. "His Majesty is well rid of the scoundrel."

"I think General Washington is a magnificent man," Georgette said. "I do not say that I think he is behaving wisely, but—"

"General? He is naught but Mr. Washington, and never forget it," Mr. Pringle interrupted. "Come to Fraunces' Tavern with us for supper and a drink." He gripped each of the young women by the arm. "Miss Grenville's parents have given their permission. I cannot imagine Miss Talbot's parents objecting."

Although Mr. Pringle maintained eye contact with Marianne, Georgette felt his thumb caressing her wrist. She pulled out of his grasp and linked hands with Mr. LaTournay again, gripping his arm for extra protection. Had her fiancé noticed? His bland expression told her nothing.

Mr. LaTournay bent to speak into her ear. "Washington's parade is nearly over anyway. Are you hungry?"

"Not hungry, but very thirsty," she admitted. "We must take Caramel home." Georgette felt somewhat guilty about her disinterest in Marianne's company, but she would have preferred to spend the remainder of the day alone with Mr. LaTournay.

He turned to the others. "We shall join you. Thank you for the invitation. First, if you will pardon the delay, I need to leave this basket at my boardinghouse. We shall take the dog home after our meal."

Mr. LaTournay's boardinghouse was located on Broadway near Trinity Church. Georgette followed Mr. Pringle and Marianne into the parlor and seated herself on a worn chair. Caramel curled up on her lap. Georgette wondered why a man of LaTournay's wealth and reputation would choose this particular boardinghouse. It seemed clean and genteel but far from luxurious. The parlor rug showed evidence of wear.

Mr. Pringle and Marianne conversed in low tones across the room, ignoring her. Marianne seemed to lose her good sense and manners in that man's presence.

The landlady popped in and straightened a vase of flowers,

all the while studying Mr. LaTournay's guests. "He's never brought people here before," she said to Georgette as if excusing her curiosity. "I always wondered if he had any friends besides his servant. He seems such a good man. 'Tis a pleasure to know he's found a fine lady to wife."

When Mr. LaTournay reappeared, Georgette felt certain he—in record time—had washed up and changed clothing. He smelled fresh; she smelled like a dust rag.

He took Caramel from her and tucked the dog under one arm. She looked up at him. "You have carried him and that basket much of the day; your arms must ache."

A smile curled the corners of his mustache. "He weighs no more than fifteen pounds." He started to say more but appeared to reconsider. "Shall we go?"

During their light supper at the tavern, Georgette caught herself yawning. Her dog slept under the table, too tired even for begging. Feeling Mr. LaTournay's gaze, she looked up and smiled. "An excess of sun and exercise has fatigued both Caramel and me, I fear."

"You will have need of a wrap before the evening ends," he said. His warm regard gave her the desire to rest her head on his shoulder.

"Should have covered up better earlier today," Mr. Pringle remarked. He reached across the table and pressed three fingers into her skin. "Look at that—she is sunburned. What a pity."

Georgette jerked her arm away. Mr. Pringle's blue eyes mocked her.

"Georgette has flawless skin. A touch of pink won't hurt this once," Marianne said. "I hope it doesn't hurt, Gigi, but at least you don't freckle."

Georgette attempted to smile, inwardly seething. If that man touched her once more, she would kick him in the shin.

When they reached the Talbots' town house, Mr. Pringle joined Mr. LaTournay in the parlor while Marianne followed

Georgette upstairs. Caramel hopped upon the bed and curled into a ball.

Georgette dropped her bonnet beside him. "Ugh, my gown is full of road dust." She gave her skirts a shake. "And neither Biddy nor Agnes is here today."

"I shall be pleased to brush it for you." Marianne unbuttoned Georgette's gown and helped her climb out of its folds. "You must have walked far today to get this dusty." She waved one hand before her face as if to dispel a cloud.

"We walked up the shore to meet the generals. You are a dear to do this for me. We shall probably meet my parents at the landing. They admire Governor Tryon." Georgette pulled out her hairpins and tried to brush dust from her hair.

"So do mine." Marianne paused with the clothes brush poised over Georgette's gown. "Gigi, are you certain Mr. LaTournay is a loyal subject of the king? At times he says things that make me uncomfortable."

Coming from Marianne, the implication annoyed Georgette. "Mr. LaTournay studies all sides of an issue before making a decision. He says we should listen and learn from wiser men than ourselves. He is admired throughout the province, Marianne." She almost told her friend that he had been introduced to General Washington but reconsidered. Marianne would not understand the tacit honor.

"I am pleased to see how fond you have become of Mr. LaTournay, dear Gigi, but I do wish you would be more discreet. You cannot know how it affects a man to have a woman touch him. Holding his hand may mean nothing to you, but that contact can mean unimaginable temptation to a gentleman, my mother says."

"If this is true, try keeping an eye on that man of yours," Georgette growled around the hairpin she held between her teeth.

A crease formed between Marianne's brows while she vigorously brushed at the gown. "Be patient with Mr. Pringle, and give the Lord time to work."

"You do not plan to marry him, I trust." Georgette stopped brushing her hair long enough to study her friend's face. "He is not good enough for you."

Marianne smiled. "You need not worry, Gigi, although you are sweet to care. I could never marry a man who did not love my Lord Jesus. Mr. Pringle knows this."

"He is insincere."

"He is a flirt," Marianne said. To Georgette's surprise, her friend's expression revealed indulgent amusement. "He tells me he originally sought me out because he heard that my father was wealthy. You see, his family business in Boston has come into hard times. But now Mr. Pringle has worked everything out with my father, who bought into the Pringle shipping business as a partner. Papa says he would rather be business partners with his future son-in-law than with anyone else."

Georgette felt stunned. "Your father has taken partnership in a failing business? Was that wise?"

"They have signed a contract with the army using Pringle ships and warehouses, you see. Papa knows a good business transaction when he sees one. Besides, he recognizes Mr. Pringle's skill with numbers and money. Mr. Pringle is smart and hardworking. He is dedicated to England and has nothing good to say about these traitors who are trying to destroy the empire. His current goal is to catch an informant they call the Frog, an infamous traitor they have reason to believe makes this city his center of operation."

"The Frog? What a ludicrous title!" Georgette's hair crackled with each stroke of the brush.

"Mr. Pringle says he is slippery and always one jump ahead," Marianne said with a smile. "I do not know who first thought up the epithet, but it seems to suit this slimy traitor. He wears a dark cloak and never shows his face. Some say he is an insane French soldier who believes he is still fighting the last war. Whatever and whoever he is, Mr. Pringle says he must be stopped."

Georgette's arm paused in midair. "Oh?"

"Mr. Pringle and two other men have set a trap to catch the Frog. Something to do with ammunition stores up in White Plains. For Mr. Pringle's sake, I pray they are successful. How he hates the rebels! Did you see his eyes flash at the mere mention of Washington? And, oh, Gigi, the truth is I love him. He makes me feel special and beautiful. When I look into his wondrous blue eyes, nothing else in the world matters at all."

"I would not have thought he could appreciate you, dear Marianne." Georgette's arm felt limp. She let it drop to her side.

"It is amazing, the changes God can make in a man's heart—or a woman's," Marianne said. "I shall be happy with my reformed scoundrel, Gigi. I know his faults and love him dearly in spite of them."

Marianne chattered about Lester Pringle's virtues while Georgette gave herself a quick sponge bath behind a screen. Out of Marianne's sight, Georgette allowed her thoughts to wander. Surely this Frog could not be her mysterious admirer. Many men wore hooded cloaks; the coincidence was too unlikely.

Marianne helped her climb back into her gown, then fluffed its skirts. Georgette pinned up her own hair. "I hope you are right about Mr. Pringle, dear Marianne," she said softly. "I would hate to see you trapped in an unhappy marriage—you, the sweetest and most unselfish of all people!"

The men rose when their two young women entered the parlor. "Thank you for waiting." Georgette handed a silk shawl to Mr. LaTournay and turned for him to drape it over her shoulders. "I hope we are not too late for the governor's parade."

Mr. LaTournay glanced at the mantel clock. "We should arrive in time. It is just down the street."

❧

Governor Tryon, a fine-looking man of military bearing, climbed the slip's steps to the foot of Broad Street and glanced around at the respectable crowd waiting to greet him. With the rest of the Loyalist crowd, Marianne and Mr. Pringle put gusto into their hurrahs. Georgette cheered hoarsely once, then fell silent, studying the people around her. Catching sight of her parents, she waved. Her mother waved back, looking more like a young girl than a matron of forty-two. Her father, on the other hand, had aged during recent months.

A salty evening breeze tugged at Georgette's bonnet. She gripped her shawl at her throat and shivered. Recalling Marianne's observation about Mr. LaTournay, she studied his face while the governor briefly addressed the crowd. He had not cheered for Tryon, but she could not recall hearing him cheer for the generals, either. Though he appeared to listen to the governor's speech, his gaze roved constantly. He seemed troubled.

Had Mr. Pringle told him about the Frog?

What would she do if Mr. Pringle captured her hero? Worse yet, what if Mr. LaTournay became involved in the pursuit? How unthinkable that her dashing admirer should be hanged or shot as a spy!

Governor Tryon and his party headed up Broad Street. Georgette turned to Mr. LaTournay. "The governor looks unhappy."

Before Mr. LaTournay could reply, Mr. Pringle rounded upon her. "And how would you feel, knowing that your city had just finished giving your opposition a welcoming parade? Did you expect him to look gratified that New York is under the control of a pack of scoundrels? He will soon set things right and punish that rabble the way he put down the Regulators when he was governor of North Carolina. You two took a risk, being seen with that mob today."

"I think not." Mr. LaTournay's voice sounded flat. "I saw

Loyalist leaders in the throng."

Mr. Pringle's blue eyes glittered. "Did you hear the news about the battle in Boston? His Majesty's troops gave that rabble militia a good thrashing and chased them off Charlestown Neck. Boston is ours again. Now Pringle Shipping can resume business and life will return to normal."

"I hope your business improves," Mr. LaTournay said.

"I am certain Mr. Grenville will also be pleased to hear the news," Georgette remarked, "since he is now a partner in your family firm. Is it true that—?"

But Mr. Pringle had already turned aside to address Marianne. Embarrassed, Georgette fell silent.

"Is what true?" Mr. LaTournay asked quietly.

"Marianne said something about Pringle Shipping signing a contract with the army. If that is true, I imagine Mr. Pringle's financial worries must now be at an end."

Mr. LaTournay looked thoughtful.

"Has he told you about the Frog?" she asked.

He focused on her face, his brow furrowed. "I believe I misunderstood. Please repeat your question."

"Has Mr. Pringle told you about the spy he intends to catch? I thought you might know about this man they call the Frog. Marianne told me of plans to trap him."

Mr. Pringle and Marianne started to join the crowd trailing the governor's retinue, then stopped and looked back. "Are you two coming?" Marianne asked.

"To be honest, since we are so near my house, I thought perhaps I would forgo this parade," Georgette said. "Please enjoy it without me." Her feet ached now even when she stood still.

"But I told my mother you and Mr. LaTournay would be with us this evening," Marianne said. "It is unseemly for me to be out alone at night with a gentleman. Did any of you happen to see my parents pass us?"

Georgette thought she saw Mr. Pringle roll his eyes, but a

moment later, he spoke reassuringly. "You will be safe with me, dearest. I am well able to protect you, if need be."

"Would you feel better, Miss Grenville, if I were to accompany you and Mr. Pringle until he leaves you at your parents' doorstep?" Mr. LaTournay offered. "I promise to be unobtrusive."

A fleeting smile touched Marianne's lips, and her lashes fluttered. Georgette could only imagine the exultation her friend must feel at the prospect of being escorted about the city by two prominent bachelors. At the moment, Georgette's feet hurt too much for her to begrudge Marianne the pleasure.

"I hardly think a chaperon will be necessary." Smiling, Mr. Pringle spoke between clenched teeth.

"I propose that you discuss the matter while we return to my house," Georgette suggested brightly. "This breeze is cool, and it begins to grow dark."

Mr. LaTournay offered her his arm. Behind them, Mr. Pringle and Marianne fell into step, arguing in muted tones. "Do you approve of my offer?" Mr. LaTournay asked quietly.

"With all my heart. I do not trust that man alone with Marianne at night."

He nodded. "I warned him away from you earlier. If he annoys you again, inform me immediately."

Georgette looked up at his shadowy face. "Thank you." Did anything escape his notice? "I enjoyed this day."

"I am gratified to hear it. I hope our future together will hold many more such days." He placed his hand over hers as they climbed the steps of her townhouse.

Again Georgette wished they were alone. He might have kissed her in the garden once more had Mr. Pringle and Marianne not joined their party.

"Business will take me out of the city these coming weeks. Use your time to prepare for our new life together." He pressed a quick kiss onto Georgette's hand. "Miss Talbot, if ever it seems I neglect you, know that such is my duty, not my desire."

Emotion filled her throat and prevented any reply. If only his stilted words rang true!

He descended the steps and joined the others. Georgette watched as Marianne took the arms of both her escorts. Their voices and laughter floated on a summer breeze.

❧

Caramel's growls awakened Georgette. Lying on her back, half asleep, she wondered what had disturbed the pug. A rattling at her window brought Caramel to his feet with a woof. Was it raining?

Georgette climbed out of bed, pulling on her bedgown as she crossed to the window. The night was clear and bright. A cloaked figure stood in the pool of light beneath a street lamp.

For an instant Georgette's blood ran cold. Her teeth began to chatter, and she clutched her gown at her throat. What to do?

Her feet took charge, carrying her swiftly downstairs and into the garden. Like a wraith, he emerged from the shadows. "I–I told you never to return," she gasped, still clasping both hands beneath her chin.

"I saw you at the parade today, *petite grenouille,* and my heart bade me try once more. Tell me you care naught for this LaTournay, this Loyalist fool."

Georgette's heartbeat thundered in her ears. That ardent voice aroused terrifying passions. "But I do care for him. I love him. Oh, how can you do this to me? It is true then—you are the Frog? They say you are insane with hatred for the English, so how can you care for me?"

"If I am insane, it is for love of you, *charmeuse.* How can you love that—that stick, that empty shell whose tongue falters unless it speaks of government, profit, and taxation? Faugh!" Turning away, he strode to a raised flower bed, propped one booted foot on its edge, and leaned his forearm on his knee.

"You do not know him as I do," Georgette replied. His

derogatory words about Mr. LaTournay cooled her ardor, arousing her protective instincts. "I want you to go. But first, because you have demonstrated kindness to me in the past, I must take this opportunity to return the favor."

The hooded head turned toward her. How tall he was, and such breadth of shoulder! She would have noticed so fine a man at the parade had she not been engrossed with Mr. LaTournay.

"Some Loyalists plan to set a trap for you. I know only that it concerns weapons or something stored in White Plains. Please, please, if you truly love me, forsake this conspiracy against the king and return to a quiet life at. . .wherever you come from."

When at last he spoke, his deep voice purred. "You do care, *ma belle.* Someday your *amoureux* shall be free to love you as you so richly deserve. Do not again risk your safety for my sake, *bien-aimée.*"

He straightened, and she took a step closer, hands pressed to her cheeks as if to stifle improper behavior. "Will I see you again?"

"You have forbidden it."

"I am to marry Mr. LaTournay."

"If I am fated to worship from afar, then God's will be done. I shall never covet another man's wife. *Adieu, Georgette.*"

A moment later she saw a dark shape atop the garden wall. Something landed at her feet. She bent to pick it up—a fragrant rose. When she looked up, he was gone.

eight

It is good that a man should both hope
and quietly wait for the salvation of the LORD.
LAMENTATIONS 3:26

After checking the identity of the visitor through a parlor window, Georgette hurried to answer a knock at the front door. "Marianne, dearest! It has been so long, nearly all summer since I saw you last." She pulled the smiling girl into the entryway and overwhelmed her with hugs. "I had feared never to see you again! I was told that your father returned to Long Island, to your family estate, while you and your mother took refuge upon a ship."

"We did, Gigi, but we plan to stay aboard only until this present crisis ends. Mama wanted to go with Papa, but he says it is not yet safe. Loyalists on Long Island are even more persecuted than we are here in the city. Today Mama and I came ashore to purchase fresh food. I begged leave to visit you, and here I am."

"Come sit down, and I shall ask Biddy to prepare coffee since we have no more tea. I baked cinnamon cakes this morning." Georgette led the way.

"You baked them? How charming!" Marianne seemed impressed.

"Biddy has been teaching me to cook and sew. I wish to be an excellent wife."

Caramel frisked about their skirts as they entered the drawing room. Georgette knew Marianne disliked animals, and it amused her to see the other girl attempt to ignore the pug's overtures of friendship.

"Caramel, come. Sit." The dog rolled to his back, but that was close enough.

"You have lost weight, Gigi. Are you well?"

"I am well enough. It is the strain. You know." Georgette gave her a significant look, and Marianne nodded. She did not need to know that Georgette's greatest strain was caused not by the threat of war but by Mr. LaTournay's extended absence. In the past month she had seen him only twice, and those visits were brief and prosaic. Her father frequently expressed the irate conviction that LaTournay's passion for Georgette had cooled, as if it were her fault.

"Tell me, how is your family? Do you see Mr. Pringle often?" In the drawing room, Georgette rang for Biddy.

"Mr. Pringle comes on a boat to visit me." Marianne's voice was too bright, and color filled her cheeks. "Papa has invited him to stay at our estate." She spread her yellow skirts on the settee. "Your wedding day rapidly approaches. Are you ready?"

"We are. It breaks my mother's heart to forgo the large reception she envisioned, but in these uncertain times, a quiet ceremony seems best."

"I am sorry for that, though I believe you are wise. May I see your gown?"

"You may. I would have liked to wear my mother's gown, but it is far away across the sea. We had this one made. It is simple brocade and satin with touches of Brussels lace at the. . . never mind. You will see it after we drink our coffee."

Biddy arrived, pushing a laden teacart. The aroma of coffee preceded her. "Why, thank you, Biddy. You anticipated our need. That will be all," Georgette said, and the elderly maid withdrew.

"Of our servants, only Biddy remains. My parents expect to sail back to England immediately after the wedding." Georgette poured the coffee and served her friend. "But I am content to travel north and leave all this talk of war behind. You will be pleased to hear that Mr. LaTournay is studying his Bible. Is that not marvelous?"

"Has he prayed to receive Christ's salvation?"

"He is a Christian. Although I do not know him well as yet, I am certain we are admirably suited. What about you, dearest? You do not seem happy."

Marianne twisted the folds of her skirt.

"What has happened? Is it Mr. Pringle? I heard unhappiness in your voice when you spoke of him earlier. Tell me," Georgette urged.

"I believe. . ." Marianne bit her lower lip and blinked hard. "I believe you were correct in your assessment of Mr. Pringle when you warned me of his insincerity. I blush to confess my wicked suspicions, but at the time I thought perhaps you were jealous that I had secured his affection. After all, he is most handsome, and at one time you thought Mr. LaTournay ugly."

The memory of her lies burned Georgette's cheeks. "What has Mr. Pringle done?"

"I sometimes hear him abuse the Lord's name, and his habit of flirting with every woman he meets has not abated with time. I tried to overlook these things, thinking the Lord would change him, but time has brought no alteration. He becomes irritable if I mention them to him, and he reminds me how faithfully he attends church. . .though he sleeps through every service. He also. . ." Her voice trailed away, and her eyes studied the floor.

Georgette patted her hand. "No need to tell me more, dear, if it makes you uncomfortable."

"But I must speak of it. I think my heart is breaking, Gigi. I did not realize how deeply I cared for him until I saw how little he truly cares for me. Mr. Pringle dotes upon me when we are together, yet I fear he forgets me as soon as we are apart. And. . . he prevailed upon me to. . . Oh, Gigi, I am so ashamed! I must marry him now, for I allowed him to kiss my lips. There. I have told you. After all my lectures to you about propriety, I have given my first kiss to a man who cares nothing for me! You must think me a woeful hypocrite."

Georgette's heart melted. "I am sure God will forgive you a momentary lapse of restraint. You will find a man worthy of your love, and Mr. Pringle will then be but a sorry memory. He is worthy of neither your love nor your regret. And your humility only makes me love you more. I am not so spotless that I should look upon you with disdain!"

No one else would ever know how often Georgette lay awake in bed at night remembering the heartbeat of her secret lover against her palms and his proclamations of undying devotion. Her pulse throbbed at any mention of revolutionary activities; always she wondered if the Frog might be involved, and she prayed daily for his safety.

Marianne shook her head. "No, I shall never find a man I could love more than Mr. Pringle. Plans are under way for our marriage, Gigi. I hope I shall have your blessing. You, of all people, know what it is to love a man despite his lack of moral principle."

"Dearest Marianne!" Wishing she had listened more and spoken less, Georgette embraced her friend.

❧

Studying Pringle's face across from the coffeehouse table, LaTournay decided his companion had lost flesh. His cheekbones protruded, and a day's growth of beard shadowed his chin. His blue eyes still flashed when he spoke of recent atrocities committed against His Royal Majesty's sovereign property. "If the Provincial Congress truly intended to replace the *Asia's* burned boat, it would have been done by now."

LaTournay sipped his coffee and swirled the dregs in his cup. "The carpenters building the second replacement boat say they were threatened."

"Precious little has been done to identify the culprits responsible for destroying both the boat and its first replacement." Pringle seemed to pulse with restrained energy. His leg jiggled beneath the table, vibrating the seat of every patron sharing his bench. "You cannot convince me that Sears and the other delegates do not know."

"If they do know, they are not telling."

Pringle's fingers drummed on the tabletop. "I want to know what they are thinking. What are they planning?"

"What makes you believe they are planning anything?"

"The very air holds tension. I have heard rumors—but then, it is not my place to speak. You will tell me if you hear anything suspicious? So far, every news item I have passed on to my superiors is old news by the time I give it."

"It cannot be profitable employment. Why have you not returned to Boston now that it is safely occupied?"

"Safely? I think not. Those raiders never sleep—burning warehouses, stealing weapons caches, taking shots at the army's guards. They must have ears everywhere."

"His Majesty's troops are invaders on foreign soil. Every tavern keeper, every serving maid, every errand boy is potentially their enemy."

Pringle sniffed. "This is civil war, not an invasion, but otherwise your observations are correct."

"You avoided my question. Why not return to Boston?"

"This life is more exciting." A hard light shone in his eyes. "We have information that may soon lead us to the Frog."

"I seem to recall hearing that exact claim more than once before."

Pringle swore. "He must have ears on every street corner."

"What has the amphibious fellow done to incite such antipathy?" LaTournay inquired. "Refuse to croak?"

Pringle apparently missed the jibe. "He cheats. Deceives. Pretends to be something he is not. I am determined to see that slippery wretch dangle from the end of a rope before I am through. I can think of no lower form of life than a spy."

"I understood you were doing investigative work for that colonel."

Pringle blinked. "Yes, but there is vast difference between a man working on behalf of the king and a traitor passing information that reveals His Majesty's army's plans to the enemy."

"I see."

After a short pause, Pringle added, "Besides, I cannot leave while Miss Grenville is aboard ship in the harbor. Her parents are planning our wedding."

"And you? Will you marry her?"

Pringle rubbed one hand down his face. "I cannot say. It should have been easy to discard the freckled creature as soon as Pringle Shipping rose from the ashes, and yet. . ." His sober expression darkened into a scowl. "There is the Grenville estate on Long Island to consider. Fine property. Slightly too rural for convenience, but its income is considerable. I am an unreformed character, mind you. No religion for me. If Miss Grenville loves me as she claims, she will take me as I am. I neither make nor demand assurances of undying fidelity."

"Marriage requires more than you are willing to give, Pringle. For Miss Grenville's sake, you should disappear and never look upon her again."

"Tell me not that you have confessed your entire past to Miss Frogface, for I shall believe none of it," Pringle mocked, visibly stung by the suggestion. "I am more honest than you, for I make no promises that I do not intend to keep." He grimaced. "Frogface. Frogs are my plague, it seems. First that slimy spy eludes my detection, and now this large-mouthed lady steals away my friend. Two of a kind they are, both destroying my happiness. I would introduce them if I could and thereby rescue you from a tragic fate. You still want me to stand up for you while you don your ball and chain next week?"

"I depend upon it. The Talbots will take ship the following day. My wife and I shall start north as soon as possible."

Pringle blurted an oath and slapped the table. "A shame it is to remove your strategic brain from the city at a time such as this. For a man with so many connections and so much influence to be wary of involvement in political affairs—it is beyond reason. The loyal citizens of New York need someone to follow, someone to help them resist and overthrow these Whig idiots. You could be that man, LaTournay. They trust you and would follow without question."

"If you believe that, Pringle, you have scant knowledge of human nature."

❧

The following day, LaTournay walked along the streets of New York, noting its atmosphere of suspense. Conditions had deteriorated during his absence. Furtive glances, hurried transactions, abandoned shops, light traffic for a fine Wednesday morning in August—the city seemed to hold its breath in fear. He had delayed too long, yet the prolonged assignation had been unavoidable.

His pace increased. Would Georgette be angry or pleased to see him? Ten days until their wedding. She undoubtedly suspected him of abandoning her. At times even he had wondered whether he would return. The wisest move would be to ship her back to England and sail after her once this conflict ended.

Mounting the front steps in two bounds, he pounded the knocker. Someone had scribbled a symbol over the door, and another ill-advised person had evidently tried to expunge it. Smeared charcoal looked even worse than the original artwork.

"Oh, Mr. LaTournay, I cannot tell you how relieved we are to see you!" Lucille Talbot clutched his sleeve and towed him into the house. "Where have you been? Georgette could tell us only that you were away on business, but what sort of business would take you from town for so long? We are in an uproar. Mr. Talbot found a merchant ship that is due to sail to England before the scheduled wedding date, and he wants to board her now."

"Why is that?"

"It is no longer safe for us here, and Mr. Talbot swears he

will not remain another week. Georgette kept telling us to wait for your advice, but you were not here to advise us, so we thought it best to pack."

Frederick Talbot joined them in the drawing room. Bags underlined his resentful eyes. "LaTournay. Hmph. We began to think you would leave our daughter at the altar." He managed to produce a fatherly tone of concern.

"And I wondered if you might be imprisoned. Have you been asked to be an officer in the traitorous army?" Lucille inquired. "I hear they have asked the sons of every important family in town. Winthrop Hardcastle, bless his heart, swore that if he were to take a commission in any army, it would be England's! My friend Myrtle Hardcastle is vastly proud of her son—yet now he has been thrown into prison, and the rest of the family has taken refuge on the *Kingfisher.*"

Talbot jumped in. "Which again brings up the question of Georgette. Mrs. Talbot and I plan to board ship as soon as possible. The *Lily Fair* leaves for England August thirtieth."

"I told him already," Lucille inserted.

"It means a precipitate wedding, if you still plan to marry our daughter."

"Mr. Talbot!" Lucille gasped. "Of course he still wishes to—" Her husband cut her off with a sharp gesture.

LaTournay studied their apprehensive faces. Their inability to return to England on any ship unless he purchased their passage remained unspoken. He disliked rewarding Talbot's manipulations, and yet. . . "If Miss Talbot is receptive to the plan, I shall not refuse."

Talbot's brow smoothed, and he beamed. "Come, my boy. Sit down and take some coffee. Lucille, pour for him."

LaTournay took a seat opposite Talbot and sipped sweetened coffee. Talbot was a well-informed man, affable and clever. However, his selfish disregard for others, particularly his wife and daughter, precluded any attachment on LaTournay's part.

The man fidgeted in his chair. "I favor summoning the

parson here and finalizing the issue today. The banks and shipping offices are open many hours yet."

"Why the haste? Has anyone threatened you?" LaTournay asked. Greatly though he desired to marry Georgette, the suggestion of coercion galled him.

"Nay, but a mob of seamen has thrown stones in the windows of several nearby houses. They attack only those people known to be loyal to the Crown, and nearly everyone knows us."

"Someone used charcoal to draw a strange black figure above our doorway. It looks like a frog to me, though Frederick claims it is an X," Lucille added.

"I saw it," LaTournay said. "Although these mobs intimidate good citizens, I have heard of them harming no one."

"But—but—the ships!" Lucille sputtered. "At any time the warships could fire upon the city and kill us all. There has been provocation for such an attack many times over. I cannot imagine why Governor Tryon waits!"

"The war ships' captains are well aware that many loyal British subjects still reside in the city, and the New York citizenry still supplies water and food to their crews. Despite the tough talk and posturing, it is highly unlikely that shots will be fired in the foreseeable future, Mrs. Talbot. A burned and gutted New York would be of no use to the British. Anyone can see that Manhattan Island could be taken at any time by a sizable landing force, for how could it be defended? The rebels have no way to prevent such an invasion. England can afford to be patient and wait for events in Boston to run their course."

"I care not what you say; it is a matter of time." Talbot leaped to his feet. "I'm off to fetch that parson. Lucille, you prepare the girl, and LaTournay, you know your part of the bargain."

Lucille put voice to LaTournay's thoughts. "Mr. Talbot, you truly intend to marry off Georgette this very day?" The mother sounded bereft.

"I do. No sense in delay."

LaTournay rose to his feet. "I must first speak with Miss Talbot."

"Fetch the girl, Lucille. Let us aim for four o'clock. That gives us time to finish packing afterward." Talbot donned his coat as he spoke.

When the front door closed behind him, Lucille and LaTournay exchanged looks. The woman's cheeks and lips were colorless. "What shall we do?" she whispered.

"Georgette must be informed. Where is she?"

"In the garden reading, I believe. I should have called her when you first arrived, but Mr. Talbot would not—"

"I shall go to her." He gave Lucille a pat on the shoulder. She burst into tears as he left the room.

He opened the garden door and stepped outside. The tableau he viewed brought a smile to his face and ease to his heart. Yes, without doubt, he wished to take Georgette Talbot as his wife.

She lay on her belly in the grass, engrossed in a book, her chin propped on one hand. A golden braid trailed along her shoulder and looped over a sleeping Caramel. Once again she had evidently dispensed with hoops, stays, bonnet, and shoes.

"Miss Talbot." He spoke softly, but she gave a little shriek and rolled to her back, staring up at him over the edge of the book clutched between her hands. Too late she tucked her feet beneath her skirts. Caramel sat up, blinking. The dog yawned, spotted LaTournay, and trotted over to greet him.

"Mr. LaTournay!" She closed the book, laid it on the grass, and sat up. "We—we were not expecting you today."

"Nevertheless, you have me today." He approached to offer assistance. She regarded his hands before placing hers within them. He hauled her up and gripped her elbows when she would have stepped away. "I must speak with you upon an urgent matter."

Her brown eyes studied his face, and she nodded.

"Your father wishes us to marry today instead of waiting

until September second. I am willing, but I would not rush you. You do understand that your parents intend to return to England immediately?"

Her attempt to draw breath resulted in several quick sobbing gasps. "Marry to–today?" He watched her eyelids flicker as she stared at the wall behind him. Abruptly, she covered her mouth with one hand and turned away. Her braid hung down her back like a thick rope, its sway reminding him of a horse's tail.

"Miss Talbot, you doubtless know that your father's conditions for our marriage included the purchase of their passage home." He attempted to clear his throat, but the lump remained, splintering his voice. "I want you to know that, if you prefer not to marry me now or ever, I am willing to purchase passage for you as well as for your parents. I desire your safety and happiness above all else."

Her reply, spoken between her fingers, scarcely reached his ears. "I am ready to make my new life with you, Mr. LaTournay."

The volatile mixture of joy and guilt felt like an explosion in his heart. "You do not understand what this new life might entail."

She folded her arms tightly, and he saw the outline of her shoulder blades through the fabric of her gown. Her voice sounded almost sharp. "Yet I do know that I want to share your future, whatever trials it may hold. God will be with us, blessing our love and commitment."

His chest heaved like a bellows, and his knees turned to jelly. "Love. Do you love me, Miss Talbot? You cannot even call me by my given name."

She spun around, followed by her swinging braid. Her eyes sparked. "When I commit my love and life to you, it will be for always, Jean-Maurice LaTournay."

His voice rasped. "So be it. I shall marry you, Georgette, and leave God accountable for the outcome."

nine

For this cause shall a man leave his father and mother, and shall be joined unto his wife, and they two shall be one flesh.
EPHESIANS 5:31

"I do." Georgette spoke her vows and felt Mr. LaTournay's grip on her hand tighten. She cast a glance at his face. He swallowed hard, and his dark eyes glistened. Not once did his attention stray from the Reverend Mowbray's sermon. His tanned face made his beard and hair seem lighter—or perhaps they were sun-bleached. Whatever he had been doing these past many weeks, he had spent much time out-of-doors.

Georgette wanted to be angry with him for his secrecy. She wanted to be cold and unattainable and make him pay for his desertion. She wanted to dream of her mysterious lover and hope he would rescue her at the last moment. During the last days of Mr. LaTournay's absence, she had imagined spurning him upon his return. In her mind he groveled at her feet and begged her forgiveness, promising never to look upon another woman if Georgette would take him back.

How could a man be wicked yet appear honorable? Georgette had only to catch sight of him and her vengeful plans faded into oblivion.

At Georgette's left side, her mother sobbed into a handkerchief. Biddy stood nearby, gaunt and dignified in gray bombazine. Georgette could not see her father on the far side of Mr. LaTournay, though she heard him clear his throat. The Reverend Mowbray's gentle voice belied his long, wrinkled face.

Georgette's head ached. Sweat dampened her wedding gown. Did Mr. LaTournay even notice her gown? She had hoped his eyes would brighten when she entered the drawing room. To her profound disappointment, he hardly glanced her way.

If only Marianne stood by her side. Marianne understood the heartbreak of loving an undeserving man.

At the minister's cue, Mr. LaTournay slipped a ruby ring upon her finger. His hands shook. The froth of neck cloth above his waistcoat also trembled. Georgette dared not look higher. He was shaking! The imperturbable Mr. LaTournay quaked like a nervous lapdog.

The minister pronounced them husband and wife. For better or for worse, Georgette was officially Mistress Jean-Maurice Antoine LaTournay. Her husband faced her while the Reverend Mowbray prayed. Mr. LaTournay's thumbs caressed the backs of her hands, and she heard him draw a shuddering breath.

Wishing to reassure him, she laid her cheek on his knuckles, then pressed their entwined hands to her heart. With all her being, she wanted to care for him and bring him happiness. As soon as the prayer ended, he would read her devotion in her eyes.

But when the minister closed his benediction, Georgette's father gripped Mr. LaTournay's arm and pulled him aside. Both men signed and sealed documents. Georgette watched as her new husband placed a wrapped parcel in her father's outstretched palm. Her father's eyes held an avaricious gleam.

Her mother tugged at her arm. "Do not embarrass your father, Georgette. His pride is injured enough without you watching this transaction. He would have preferred offering a dowry for you to accepting a bride price."

Although Georgette suspected the reverse, she obediently looked away. The warmth began to drain from her heart.

"Now that that is over, we'll have Georgette's trunk loaded

into the carriage." Her father clapped his son-in-law on the shoulder and winked at Georgette. "Unless you plan to stay here tonight. You two might assist with our travel preparations since you'll have nothing better to do."

The more jocular her father became, the colder Mr. LaTournay's response. "We shall lodge at my boardinghouse."

The realization that she was leaving her parents' home, never to return, struck Georgette to the heart. She looked at her mother's tearstained face, studied her father's smug expression, and felt like choking. Was this their final parting? And Juliette—would she ever see her sister again? "What about Caramel?" Her question ended on a sob.

Her father stared as if she had lost her senses. "Her dog," Mr. LaTournay explained. He took Georgette's clammy hand and squeezed it gently. "You and I shall travel north in a few days by horseback and river. I plan to send my man Noel ahead with our baggage. It will be easier for Caramel to travel with him. Noel is kind; Caramel will like him."

Georgette felt her jaw quiver. "He will be afraid. He will think I have deserted him."

"Not for long. Think how pleased he will be when you join him at Haven Farm. It would be best to leave him here overnight. Noel will collect him along with your remaining trunks in the morning."

"Yes, dear," her mother added, taking Georgette's other hand. "Biddy will be packing up your remaining belongings tonight. She will pack everything your pet will need, I am certain. You go ahead and leave everything to me."

"All this bother about a dog. Dump the beast in the river and have done," her father huffed. "I must drive the parson home now. Oh." He paused and pulled a folded note from his waistcoat. "Nearly forgot to give you this. It arrived this morning. From the Grenville girl. Good night, Daughter. Be a good wife if you know how and make your husband happy. We shall speak our farewells on the morrow, I've no doubt."

Watching him escort the minister outside, Georgette wondered if her father had ever loved her.

The carriage driver stood in the hall just outside the parlor. "You got a trunk I should carry out?" He ducked his head in a bow and twisted his hat between his hands. His widening eyes took in Georgette's gown.

"The one in the hallway at the head of the stairs," her mother said.

Mr. LaTournay headed upstairs, and the driver stumped after him. "God's blessings on you and your new missus," Georgette overheard the burly man say. " 'Pears to me like you done married an angel."

Her mother closed the parlor door and embraced her. "Darling, I shall miss you so! I never wanted it to be this way. Juliette had a lovely wedding with many guests, but this!" Fresh sobs wracked her frame.

"It was not your doing, Mummy. I know you wanted a fancy wedding for me, but the husband matters far more than the ceremony. I do love my husband, and I believe we shall be happy together."

She broke the seal, unfolded her note, and read quickly.

Dearest Gigi,

My conscience will give me no rest since I visited you the other day. You must be told. Both my mother and I have seen Mr. LaTournay aboard this ship in the company of Lady Forester, once late at night, and never when her husband was near. Please do not hate me. My heart breaks for you as yours does for me.

Marianne

Georgette folded the note.

"What is wrong, dearest? Is Marianne unwell?"

Georgette handed her the letter. She scanned the page and sighed. "Alas, I had hoped you would not hear of this so soon."

Georgette gaped. "You knew? You knew and did not tell me?"

Her mother would not meet her gaze. "I feared you would refuse to marry him. You know how essential it is for your father and me to return to England, Georgette. Any further delay would ruin us. You must learn to tolerate men and their weaknesses, my dear. Such things are part of life. But you will find compensation if you seek it." She dabbed her tears away with a soggy handkerchief. "I always have."

Regaining control, she wagged a finger in Georgette's face. "Marriage is for babies and security. Love is another thing altogether."

Georgette wandered to the front window and stared out at the street. Her chest heaved in the effort to maintain control. Waves of heat rose from the cobblestones. Muggy air blanketed the city—it seemed worlds away from a crisp spring night, sparkling stars, and romance. Right there, beneath that street lamp, the Frog had waited, looking up at her window. His avowal of undying love rang in her memory. She had sent him away forever. Even if by chance her mysterious hero were now to appear, he would be too late to rescue her.

❧

LaTournay stared blankly at passing buildings and trees as the hired carriage rolled along the street. Not until he spoke them aloud had the full meaning of his wedding vows struck home. *Until death do us part.* Would he have the chance to grow old with Georgette? Would ever the day come when she knew him fully and loved him without measure? Or would his entire life be a lie, a charade, lived in craven fear of her ultimate rejection?

Georgette deserved better.

He turned to regard his wife's profile and noted her pallor. "Georgette, are you well?"

She gave him a weak smile, and regret twisted in his gut. Her wedding day, yet she looked frightened and ill. "My head aches, likely due to the heat," she said. "When did you say we shall travel north?"

"If you are well enough, I had thought to leave Saturday morning. My business in town is complete." He forced his voice to remain calm and sympathetic. "If you wish, you might rest your head upon my shoulder."

Eyes closed, she relaxed against his shoulder. Despite his concern for her health, LaTournay felt excitement stir within him. For weeks and months, he had denied himself the pleasure of her embrace—had denied even the thought of her kisses. Duties had kept his mind and body occupied, and determination kept his imagination from straying into forbidden grounds.

Would she welcome his attentions?

His valet, Noel Dimieux, greeted them at the door to LaTournay's apartments. A smile nearly split the man's wrinkled brown face. Georgette acknowledged the introduction and thanked Noel for his congratulations. LaTournay ushered his wife into the sweltering sitting room. The windows stood wide but caught no ocean breezes. Moisture beaded on Georgette's pallid face and dampened the ringlets at her temples. Her hands trembled as she attempted to untie her bonnet strings.

"If you want to remove that gown, the bedchamber is beyond that door," LaTournay said before realizing how she might misunderstand. He tugged at his tightening collar. "Your trunk is there. If you like, I shall request to have a bath brought up."

Georgette nodded. "A bath would be nice."

❧

While Georgette bathed, LaTournay paced the sitting room, flopped into a chair, and rose to pace again.

Noel laid a light supper, then prepared to withdraw. He spoke in French. "A message left for you not yet an hour past, monsieur." He handed over a twisted paper.

With muttered thanks in the same language, LaTournay frowned as he untwisted the note. Its contents darkened his frown. *"Folie."* Crushing it in one hand, he tossed it upon the hearth.

He sensed Noel's regard but refused to acknowledge the silent inquiry. "That will be all, Noel."

"Oui, monsieur. God bless you and Madame LaTournay."

"What do you think of my wife?"

"Who could not approve such a fine woman, monsieur? *Très belle.* I now understand your determination to wed the lady." Noel failed to conceal a fatherly smile. "Be patient with her, monsieur. I believe she suffers from emotional exhaustion—a common malady of new brides."

"Ah." The unsolicited advice startled him, coming from reticent Noel. *"Merci."*

"I shall prepare your people at home for madam's arrival," Noel promised with a toothy grin. "And you may assure madam that I will attend her dog as if it were my own. I shall enjoy meeting the animal again. God's richest blessings on your marriage, monsieur."

For nearly an hour after Noel's departure, LaTournay read the newspaper, stared out the window, or paced. More than once he started to knock upon Georgette's chamber door, then reconsidered. At last he could wait no longer. "Georgette?"

Silence.

He opened the door. Evening shadows dimmed the small chamber, but he could see her clothing heaped upon the floor. Soap filmed the water in the unoccupied tub. Georgette lay prone upon the bed, clad in something white. Her golden hair cloaked her shoulders and most of her face. LaTournay knelt and touched her forehead. Damp and warm, but not feverish. He let his hand slide the length of her hair, down her back to her waist.

She moaned and her eyelids fluttered. "Mr. LaTournay. . . so sorry. My head. . ."

"Hush." He dipped a handkerchief in the tepid water in his basin, wrung it out, and pressed it upon her forehead. Soon she slept again, her expression more relaxed.

LaTournay ate a lonely supper of cheese, bread, and sliced fruit. While prowling about his apartments, he cast occasional glances at the activity in the lamp-lit street below. Though the hour grew late, men headed toward the southern tip of the island, singly and in groups. LaTournay shook his head, refusing to believe, and turned away.

Shouts from below brought him to the window again. What he saw raised the hair at his nape. Making no effort at concealment, dozens of men hauled cannons up Broadway, grunting and groaning as they dragged at the heavy ropes. In defiance of reason, the rebels proceeded with their plot to purloin British cannons from the Grand Battery at Fort George.

LaTournay checked on Georgette. Candlelight revealed her peaceful face, turned her hair to a curtain of gold, and shimmered amid the silken folds of her garment. She would not notice his brief absence. Better to be occupied than to brood upon his wife's temporarily inaccessible charms.

While changing into dark woolen garments, he pondered the repercussions to this provocative move by the Provincial Congress. The British must be aware of the rebels' movements. Until now, they had displayed remarkable forbearance with the Americans, but blatant thievery of sovereign property was another matter.

Leaving his candle behind, he slipped into the dark hallway and down the stairs.

❧

Boom! The first earthshaking explosion pierced Georgette's fuzzy dreams. Several more salvos in rapid succession brought her eyes wide open. Darkness met her gaze. Shouts of panic reached her ears. "What was that? Where am I?" she asked aloud, struggling to sit upright. "What time is it?"

She sat upon a bed, clad in the scanty satin chemise her

mother had insisted would be ideal for her wedding night. Wedding. She was a married woman. Memories of the ceremony flitted through her mind.

At least her head no longer ached.

"Mr. LaTournay?" She dimly recalled him bathing her forehead with cool rags, but that was all. She must have fallen asleep.

A thin line of light showed beneath the door. He must be in the other room. She groped around in the dark but could not find a bed gown. No matter. What had caused the noise outside? Was the city under attack? No further explosions had ensued, but now drums began to pound. Someone inside the boardinghouse screamed, and Georgette's heart thudded.

"Jean-Maurice?" Shoving open the door, she almost fell into the sitting room. A candle burned upon a table in the deserted chamber.

Georgette rubbed her bare arms. Perhaps her husband had stepped outside for a moment. Surely he would not desert her on their wedding night. Taking the candle back to the bedchamber, she located her lace bedgown. Mr. LaTournay must have removed the tub and straightened the room while she slept.

She dared to peer down into the street through an open window. A number of large wheeled objects—cannons?—lined Broadway. Men appeared to be towing them north toward the common, using ropes. The street lamps revealed other people throwing their possessions into wagons, handcarts, and wheelbarrows. Many rushed along the street. Voices and traffic blended into a cacophony. Mounted horses pushed through the crowds, endangering pedestrians. Fear thickened the night air.

Feeling helpless, Georgette plopped upon the settee, nibbled at her stale supper, and watched the candle burn low. Should she dress herself and prepare for flight? If she were in any danger, Mr. LaTournay would return for her. He might be fighting even now to save New York from annihilation. Haven Farm suddenly sounded like heaven. "We must leave this dreadful place," she told the candle.

Her eyelids drifted shut despite the commotion outside. She awakened with a cry as flashes illuminated the room and explosions shook the night. *Boom, boom, boom*—one after another, in seemingly endless succession. An eerie whistle and a crash, sounding horribly close, followed each shot. Clapping both hands over her ears, Georgette slid to the floor and sobbed in panic. "Lord God, save us!" Could this be the end of the world?

Quick steps rang on the hardwood floor and strong hands pulled her into a secure embrace. "Georgette." Mr. LaTournay spoke between the blasts, making fervent entreaties to God. Scratchy wool rubbed her forehead and shoulders as she burrowed into her husband's chest. Lying beside her on the rag rug, he sheltered her with his body.

At last the barrage ceased. Outside, the city's stunned populace continued to wail and shout. "What was it?" Georgette whispered. Her candle must have expired, for the room was dark.

"The *Asia,* I would guess, expressing her captain's displeasure concerning the removal of His Majesty's cannons from the Battery. Stay down, my dear. I shall check for possible fires." He scrambled to his feet, and Georgette immediately wished him back. His silhouette appeared at the window.

"I see no flames, and no alarm has been sounded. I imagine the purloined cannons will remain where they are for the present. It was a foolish attempt, at any rate."

"The *Asia* fired upon us? Upon our city? But why? We might have been killed!" Georgette could not stop trembling.

"And yet the Lord has preserved us this night, my wife. You shiver. Come to bed; I believe it will be safest to remain here for the night. Chaos reigns in the streets below. I returned to you with difficulty." He pulled her to her feet.

"But where did you go? You left me here alone?"

"I intended to step outside for only a moment. The folly of that plan is now clear to me, but at the time it seemed wise. You slept, and I meant to return before you knew of my absence. I apologize, Georgette. I was wrong to leave you unprotected."

"Why did you wait so long to return?" Her teeth chattered.

"I attempted to come back after the first shots were fired, but a crowd of panicked humanity pushing me in the opposite direction delayed my return. The ferries must be inundated."

"My parents! Are they safe?"

"We cannot tell until morning. You must entrust them to God's care." He put his arm across her shoulders and guided her toward the bedchamber.

"What time is it?"

"Past three o'clock." He turned back the coverlet while Georgette slipped off her bedgown. Although the room was dark, she felt shy about climbing into bed in his presence. He tucked the coverlet around her. "Warm enough?"

"Mr. LaTournay, were you in this city last week?"

A pause. "I was sometimes in the vicinity. Why do you ask?"

"You were seen visiting Lady Forester on one of the merchant ships." The strength of her own voice amazed her. The truth could not be worse than her doubts.

"I did not board the ship intending to visit her."

"Then why were you there?"

"Conducting business. I am a merchant; it was a merchant ship. I spoke to Lady Forester only of business." His voice held the ring of truth.

"If you were in the vicinity, why did you not visit me?" She tried but failed to sound unconcerned.

"I have labored to complete my work in this area so that I may enjoy many uninterrupted months at home with my wife during the winter. My desire would be never to return here, though I fear this will prove impossible." His voice deepened. "I dreamed of you every night, Georgette."

Her eyes closed as passion flooded her veins. She longed to believe him. This was no time to reconsider the consequences of her decisions. A godly wife had but one choice.

"Now I am here," she said. "Are you not coming to bed? You must sleep, too."

"If you wish it."

She heard the rustle of fabric and a moment later felt him slide beneath the coverlet beside her. Fear vanished, leaving breathless excitement in its wake. "I am sorry for falling asleep earlier. My head ached so, I could not bear it."

"It no longer aches?"

"Due to your tender care, Jean-Maurice. Will you hold me again?" She scooted over, and his eager arms drew her close.

❧

The following afternoon, Georgette's parents hugged her good-bye and shook hands with their new son-in-law. "So the warships will not fire upon New York in the foreseeable future, eh?" her father said, savoring Mr. LaTournay's error one last time. Georgette had lost count hours ago of repetitions on the same theme.

"I thought I should die of fear," her mother said. "If only we had taken ship yesterday! Mr. LaTournay, I trust you will hurriedly remove our daughter to safety. I shudder to think of her in this treacherous city."

"I shall endeavor to protect my wife to the best of my ability, Mrs. Talbot. We covet your prayers on our behalf."

"And you shall have them." She hugged Georgette one last time, then allowed her husband to help her into the *Lily Fair*'s boat. Burly seamen applied the oars, and the boat slipped into the open harbor.

Georgette wiped away fresh tears and waved until the tiny figures disappeared from her sight. "Will they be safe, do you think?"

"Safer than we are here." Mr. LaTournay slipped an arm around her waist. She leaned into his chest and let a few tears dampen his waistcoat, grateful for his strong embrace.

"I wish we could leave today for Haven Farm." She wanted away from this horrible city surrounded by warships. Away from the drilling militia and ranting newspapers. Away from other women who might try to steal her husband.

"Saturday will be better. We shall soon be home, my wife."

Although they stood on the slip in public view, Georgette pressed closer to his side. "May we return home now?"

"Home?"

"To our boardinghouse. My home is wherever you are."

He wrapped her in a warm hug. Georgette could not bother to worry about her husband's past nor concern herself about the future. The present was enough.

ten

Every wise woman buildeth her house:
but the foolish plucketh it down with her hands.
PROVERBS 14:1

"We are nearly home. Do you see the house?" Mr. LaTournay pointed ahead. "The large white building surrounded by elms."

"I see it." After days of travel by boat and horseback, Georgette was more than ready to settle in at Haven Farm. However, the thought of meeting her new family while in this bedraggled state held little appeal.

"The house on our left belongs to my sister, Francine, and her husband, Jan. There she is—Francine!" Mr. LaTournay waved an arm above his head and urged his tired horse into a canter. Georgette's gray gelding followed.

The woman in the doorway waved back and ran toward them down the sloping green lawn surrounding her house. Two dogs barked and leaped about her skirts. A flock of geese ran honking in the opposite direction.

"I thought you would never get here!" she shouted. "Welcome to Haven Farm, Georgette!" As the horses slowed, Francine fell into step between them and laid her hand on Georgette's knee, beaming an irresistible smile. "Did you have a *bon voyage?* You must be exhausted! Yvonne—she is Noel's wife—has prepared supper up at the big house. First you can have a hot bath, and—"

"Is a brother now beneath your notice? Or am I invisible?" Mr. LaTournay demanded.

Francine turned. "Hello to you, too, Jean-Maurice. I hope

your wife keeps you from wasting another winter." She gave Georgette a grin. "Georgette, I cannot express my gratitude to you for marrying *mon frère.* Jan and I thought he might pine himself to death last year on account of you."

Georgette gave Mr. LaTournay a startled glance. He rose in his stirrups to study something across the fields, ignoring the remark. "Would you like a quick tour of the farm on horseback?" he asked.

"I would prefer to see the farm another time. I am tired." That promised hot bath beckoned.

"Of course you are. Jean-Maurice is not thinking clearly. He should know better." Francine patted Georgette's horse. "A fine animal this is."

"Royal was a gift to me from Mr. LaTournay," Georgette said. "I am pleased to meet you, Francine." Her return greeting felt awkward, coming so late in the conversation.

Francine smiled up at her again. "I am pleased to have a sister after all these years. May I call you Georgie?"

Georgette tried to conceal her horror. "My friend Marianne calls me Gigi."

"Gigi? *Eh, bien.* My husband, Jan, asked me to extend his apologies for not greeting you yet; he will join us this evening." Francine gave Royal's sweaty neck another pat and stopped, allowing the horses to pass as she called after them. "I shall give you time to settle in, Gigi, but later you will tire of my company. Yvonne and I have joyfully anticipated the arrival of another woman!" She waved and trotted back toward her house.

"Francine seems an exuberant woman," Georgette observed. "I think I shall enjoy her company." She read approval in her husband's smile.

A young black man emerged from the barn to take the horses, greeting Mr. LaTournay in rapid French. He extended a sealed note.

Mr. LaTournay thrust the letter inside his waistcoat without a glance. "Thank you. Georgette, this is Pierre Dimieux, son of Noel and Yvonne. Pierre, my wife."

Pierre smiled, bowed, and spoke in perfect English. "Welcome, Mrs. LaTournay. I pray you will be happy here at Haven Farm."

Georgette nodded. "Thank you, Pierre."

Mr. LaTournay hopped lightly to the ground. "Please give the horses both a good rubdown tonight. The new gelding belongs to Mrs. LaTournay."

"*Oui,* monsieur. He is handsome." Pierre held the horse while Georgette dismounted. She handed over the reins with relief, wondering if she would ever again be able to walk normally.

Pierre questioned Mr. LaTournay in rapid French. This time her husband replied sharply in French. Pierre's expression darkened. Not for the first time, Georgette wished she knew more of the language.

As her husband took her arm and escorted her from the barn, she asked, "Is anything wrong?"

"Nothing that need concern you." He looked up at the house, and his face brightened. "Your home, Madame LaTournay."

Georgette thought it looked like a barn with windows, but she dared not voice that opinion. "I have never before seen such a house."

"It is gambrel style. Dutch. My grandfather built it." He reached inside to unlatch the lower half of the door.

"Why are the doors split in half?"

"So we can let light and air into the house without also allowing hogs, dogs, and geese inside. All the outer doors are that way." Suddenly he scooped her into his arms and pushed the door with his foot. Gasping at the suddenness of his move, Georgette clutched at his neck.

"Now this I like to see," a rich female voice said from inside the house.

"Bonjour, Yvonne." Mr. LaTournay sounded at once embarrassed and exultant. Georgette looked up to see a woman with dark skin, gray-streaked hair, and white teeth.

"Très bien to have you home, and the new madam, too!" The woman wiped her hands on her apron.

Mr. LaTournay set Georgette down, keeping one arm wrapped around her waist. "Georgette, meet our housekeeper and friend, Yvonne Dimieux. Yvonne, this is Georgette, my wife."

Georgette nodded. "I am pleased to meet you, Yvonne."

Yvonne bobbed a curtsy.

"Yvonne grew up in Tobago; she dislikes our northern winters. She is an excellent cook and housekeeper, so every autumn I must convince her to stay."

Yvonne grinned. "Liar that you are, monsieur. The Lord Jesus keeps me and Noel here with you. We will never go where He does not lead." Without pausing for breath, she added, "Bath water heats in the kitchen, and the tub awaits madam in her chamber. You speak the word, and I'll send the boys up with the hot water. The beds are turned, the linens fresh. I shall unpack for madam while she rests. I have something of hers in the kitchen. I'll bring it with me when I come upstairs."

"Merci, Yvonne."

All this French talk startled Georgette. Of course she had known that Mr. LaTournay spoke French, but now it seemed to flow from his tongue and accent even his English.

The housekeeper's dark eyes twinkled. "If you do not realize it already, madam, this husband of yours speaks only half his thoughts and even fewer of his feelings. You must make the man talk." With a nod and a wink, she whirled about and left.

Bemused by the advice, Georgette stared up at her husband's face.

Stepping back, Mr. LaTournay smiled. "Yvonne has wisdom to equal her remarkable intellect and a loving heart like none other. Now, be at home and do whatever you wish. This house is yours, Georgette. You have first bath. I shall join you upstairs later."

"You will read your letter?"

He seemed startled by the question. "*Oui.* The letter. I shall read it, of a certain."

❧

Yvonne delivered Georgette's possession to her bedchamber. "For you, madam. He was asleep on the hearth when you arrived."

"Caramel!" Georgette held out her arms.

The pug's floppy ears lifted at the sound of her voice, and he struggled to get down. As soon as Yvonne placed him on the floor, he yipped and spun in circles near Georgette's feet. "I do believe he is crying," Georgette said, attempting to hold the frantic dog. Tears of relief burned her eyes. The pug looked hearty and plump; Noel had truly been good to him. Georgette had trained Caramel not to lick her face; but when she picked him up, his tongue darted in and out near her cheek as if to taste the air.

Yvonne watched the reunion with an enigmatic smile. "He will be a piece of your past to soothe your heart," she said.

Georgette's first impressions of her new home were of large, clean rooms with wooden beams and white walls, immense fireplaces, and handsome furnishings. She felt pampered by Yvonne, who bathed her, combed out her hair, and helped her dress for supper as if she were a princess. She found the woman's stream of accented conversation soothing, laced with tales of Jean-Maurice and Francine as children. She helped Georgette unpack and arrange her clothing and possessions.

"*Voyons,* but you have lovely things!" Yvonne stepped back to admire her handiwork. The room looked bright and homey with Georgette's possessions scattered about. Caramel had already claimed the rug on the hearth.

"I hope there is room for Mr. LaTournay's things," Georgette said. "My gowns take up so much space."

"Monsieur uses the adjoining bedchamber as his dressing room. Never you worry," Yvonne said. "This house has rooms and to spare for you and a brood of children."

Georgette tried to ignore that last comment. "Does Noel help him dress?"

"The master claims no need of a valet when he is home, so Noel helps me keep the household in order. Come to supper when you are ready."

Yvonne opened the door to reveal Mr. LaTournay in the hallway. He stepped back, allowing the housekeeper to pass, then entered Georgette's room. Caramel gave him a cheerful greeting, rolling on his polished shoes to beg a belly rub.

"You look fine," Georgette said. Her husband had changed into a blue coat, brocaded waistcoat, and buff breeches. His unpowdered hair was brushed into a neat queue.

He scanned the room. "Does this bedchamber meet with your approval? You may choose another if it does not suit."

"It is most satisfactory. Of a certain, I must adjust to sleeping in a cave."

He glanced at the alcove bed. "It is warm in winter. You will see."

"I am sure I shall. I also see that I needn't have packed my featherbed. You must own many, since my bed frame already holds two." She crossed to the window and gazed upon rolling, forested hills and green pastureland already wearing a tint of autumn color. Cattle and sheep dotted the fields. "The view is particularly fine."

His hands slipped around her waist from behind, and she melted against his chest. His breath and lips against her temple brought a relieved sigh. As long as Mr. LaTournay loved her, she could endure.

"You are wonderful, my Georgette. They all love you, as I knew they would. Come, we must go down for our wedding supper. Yvonne has prepared a feast in your honor."

"She is kind, Jean-Maurice, as are Noel and Francine."

"Are your fears relieved?"

"Most of them. You will not leave me alone tonight?"

"You need to ask?" He kissed her before escorting her downstairs.

❧

The outside world seldom touched Georgette's little paradise of Haven Farm that autumn of 1775. She diligently applied herself to ignoring the few concerns marring her happiness. True, the town church's minister was an unabashed proponent of the rebel cause, but he seldom allowed his political views to color his sermons. Talk of war filtered through town, and Georgette knew of several local families whose sons had joined the traitorous army, yet these things she could disregard.

One afternoon in November, Francine dropped by to give Georgette a weaving lesson. "Before we settle down to work, I would really like a refreshment," Francine said, linking arms with her new sister. "I hear via family gossip that Yvonne is teaching you to cook and clean house." She stepped back to allow Georgette to enter the hall first, since their two hoop skirts could not simultaneously fit through the doorway.

"I must have something to fill my days—"

"Non, my dear sister, you misunderstand. I approve of your activity, as does *mon frère."* Her bright smile soothed Georgette's ruffled feelings. "Yvonne abandoned training me years ago, but enough of her skill soaked through my thick skull that Mr. Voorhees finds me a satisfactory cook."

A stack of letters on the hall table caught Georgette's eyes. She stopped to examine the addresses. "Mr. LaTournay writes and receives many letters."

Francine gave her a speculative look. "He is a busy man. Too busy, in the opinion of some. Not busy enough, in the opinion of others."

"So many letters addressed to my husband; none for me. Does mail no longer travel to England?" Georgette dropped the letters back on the table. "My parents must have received at least one of my letters by this time. Why do they not reply? And why does Marianne never write to me?"

Francine shook her head and looked sympathetic as she towed Georgette into the kitchen. At the worktable, Yvonne chopped vegetables with a huge cleaver. Bundles of onions, garlic, and herbs hung from the ceiling, and a great kettle steamed over a crackling fire.

"Would either of you like some cider?" Francine made herself at home in the great house.

Yvonne smiled and refused without breaking rhythm.

"Gigi?"

"Please." Georgette brooded over troubling thoughts. "Farming must be stressful work. Often Mr. LaTournay looks tired and troubled. Sometimes. . ."

"Sometimes?" Francine poured two pewter mugs full of cider.

"When we read the Scriptures together, certain passages seem important to him, yet he cannot explain why. We read a story about a man named Gideon the other day, and Mr. LaTournay asked me to read it aloud twice. He has spoken of it several times since. Is your husband mysterious like that?"

"Jean-Maurice is more mysterious than most. Has he told you about his childhood?" Careful to keep out of Yvonne's way, the ladies sat upon a settle near the open hearth.

"Very little. He seldom speaks of the past. I know he was born in Canada and spoke French as his first language. I know that your father was French and your mother part Dutch. You both lived here for many years, so I assume your father died young."

"Papa was a French soldier—Claude-Albert Francois LaTournay, handsome, romantic, and silver-tongued. Grandfather disapproved of him, but Maman ran away to marry him and regretted it ever after. Papa took her to Canada with him until he tired of being husband and father. He brought Maman here when we were children and left us in Grandfather's care."

"How sad she must have been!" Georgette mourned the disillusioned young mother.

"Our mother tried to shield us from knowledge of our father's perfidy, but he made his own character known to us later. During the Indian wars, he returned to claim Jean-Maurice. Mercifully, he left me here with Grandfather."

"Your mother died?"

"The year before our father's return. Jean-Maurice was thirteen when she died, and he missed her terribly. He still mourns her loss, I believe. Before Maman's death, he was a mischievous boy, always in trouble yet smart enough to talk his way out of punishment. Her death took all the fun out of his life."

"He seldom smiles." Georgette sipped her cider, trying to imagine Mr. LaTournay as a lanky young boy.

"I have never seen him happier than he has been these last few months."

Georgette smiled. "That is good to hear. Sometimes I wonder how he can be pleased with me. You know how hopeless I am at any profitable chore. He might have married any one of a dozen other accomplished young ladies in Saratoga alone, not to mention the hordes of females yearning after him in New York."

"I shall let Jean-Maurice assure you of his undying love. Enough for me to say that he paid heed to no woman but his mother until you came along."

Georgette winced inwardly. Mr. LaTournay's dissolute reputation remained unknown at Haven Farm, and she had no wish to disillusion his family.

"His sun rises and sets on you, *Gigi fille,*" Francine continued. "I would not wish to be wife to such a man, but you are the ideal woman for *mon frére.* You possess courage and tenacity. Loving Jean-Maurice for a lifetime will require both."

Confused, Georgette shook her head. Perhaps Francine knew of her brother's moral failings after all. "I am sure it must be as difficult for him to love me as it is for me to love him."

"*J'en doute.* Behind every great man stands an even greater woman, if you want my opinion," Francine said. "You be Deborah to his Barak, support him fully, and you will reap rich rewards. It is not my place to tell you things he chooses to keep secret, but I shall let you know that Jean-Maurice undergoes a struggle."

"Involving me?"

"*Certainement.* When principle strives against passion. . ." Francine paused and smiled. "It is time for me to hold my tongue. You cannot know how tempted I am to divulge certain facts. I say it is high time he told you many things about himself, but does he listen to me? Ha!"

❧

LaTournay stamped his boots on the stoop to remove muck and snow. Once inside the lean-to, he took off the filthy boots and hung up his overcoat. The stench of livestock clung to his clothing and skin. He could not greet Georgette while smelling like manure. Stocking-footed, he ran up the back stairs to his dressing room. A fire burned on the hearth in anticipation of his arrival.

The water in his basin was tepid, but it felt good on his chilled body. He toweled warmth into his skin and dressed quickly. Somewhere in this barn of a house, Georgette awaited his coming. Her eyes would brighten at sight of him, and she would greet him with a kiss.

"Jean-Maurice?"

"I am here." He ran a comb through his damp hair.

She opened the door between their rooms. "Francine was here today to teach me weaving." Georgette wore a gown he particularly admired, pink and white like her skin. Wisps escaped her upsweep of hair. Her welcoming smile was as warm and inviting as he had anticipated.

"I was dirty." He reached to tie off his pigtail with a string.

"You smell nice now." Just as he had hoped, her hands slid up his chest. "And you feel nice." Wonder of wonders, she returned his fascination and delight in equal measure. Would he ever tire of her soft form and loving embrace? A man would have to be dead.

The string fell to the floor, unnoticed.

❧

That night after Scripture reading, Georgette asked, "Jean-Maurice, why were you so sad when first we met?" She shifted the sock she was knitting and dropped the ball of yarn on the floor. Caramel picked it up and started to trot away. "No, Caramel, drop it!" she cried.

LaTournay caught the dog and retrieved the yarn. After a quick search, he located the dog's basket of playthings and selected a shredded leather ball. "Here, young fellow. Play with this."

"Thank you." Georgette tucked the yarn ball beneath her elbow. "Perhaps 'sad' is not the correct description. Your eyes held such emptiness, such unspeakable sorrow, as if. . ."

He tossed the ball for Caramel and watched the dog scrabble on the floorboards. "Speak on." The pit of his stomach felt hollow. He settled back in his chair and crossed one ankle over the other.

"As if you had looked upon hell itself."

He leaned down to tug the slimy ball from Caramel's mouth and threw it again. "You spoke of me with Francine today."

She tipped her head quizzically. Firelight danced in the hollows and curves of her face and throat. "I wish to know everything about you, Jean-Maurice. You are the favored subject of my conversation and my dreams. Does this annoy you?"

Her increasing perceptiveness with regard to his thoughts

and emotions could become inconvenient. "Anything you wish to know, ask me, not Francine." He tried to keep his tone light.

"What happened when your father came back for you? Francine says he left her behind and took you with him. It must have been difficult for you to leave this place. Did you even remember your father, or was he a stranger to you?"

He focused on Caramel, letting the little dog wrestle him for the ball. Les Pringle's warnings about women flashed through his mind, followed by proverbs about bothersome wives. Why could she not be content in her ignorance?

"I think I did remember him vaguely. But now I am here, married to the loveliest woman in all America." He rose and moved behind her chair to rub her neck and shoulders.

She dropped her knitting to clasp his hands and look up with adoring eyes. "Are you content as a farmer, Jean-Maurice? Sometimes I cannot help wondering. You often seem troubled. I enjoy discussing the Scriptures with you each night, but I cannot match your depth of understanding. You are so intelligent and gifted; it seems wicked to waste your talents upon dumb animals and a simple wife."

For a moment he wondered how it would feel to grant her admission to his deepest thoughts and feelings. But sharing his complete history was unthinkable. She must remain content with the portion of his life he was able to share.

Bending, he kissed her neck. "Have I complained about your conversation?" He parried question with question. "I enjoy discussing Samson, Gideon, Moses, and our other historical friends each night. I respect your knowledge of Jesus Christ."

"I know you read the Scriptures on your own. You insist upon reading the Bible straight through when we read together, but you have been peeking ahead into New Testament books. I know because you have moved my markers. I wish you would discuss those passages with me as well as the Old Testament stories."

Taken by surprise, he muttered, "I am unprepared to discuss them."

When he tried to pull his hands away, she tightened her hold. "Jean-Maurice, if you are a Christian, God has forgiven whatever sins you committed in the past. And I could better demonstrate love to you if I knew more about you. Share with me these memories that haunt you, please? I believe it would help if you spoke of them."

He pulled his hands from her grasp as terror darkened his vision. Chest heaving, he swore in French. "You know not what you ask. Leave the past alone. Be content with the man I am; forget the man I used to be. We are happy here together, and I would keep it so. Do you understand?"

Turning away, he retreated to the adjoining room to prepare for bed. He almost decided to sleep in the smaller bed in the alcove of his chamber, but the memory of Georgette's bewildered expression brought him back to her. Shivering, he climbed beneath the covers and waited for her to join him. When she did climb into bed, he pulled her close with her back against his chest. Nuzzling into her neck, he tried to relax and absorb her sweetness. She did not resist him, but he sensed her sorrow like a barrier between them.

eleven

A time to love, and a time to hate;
a time of war, and a time of peace.
ECCLESIASTES 3:8

Georgette awakened to darkness, her heart racing. Jean-Maurice thrashed and cried out. His fist struck her arm. Still disoriented from sleep, she struggled to sit up. "Jean-Maurice, you are dreaming. Wake up."

He emitted a snarl like an animal's. Georgette yelped in fright. Braving the cold, she climbed out of bed and held a taper to the banked coals of last night's fire. Wax dripped on the hearth before the wick caught. Her husband still moaned and gasped for breath. Cupping the flame, Georgette set the candle in a holder and placed it on the bedside table. "Jean-Maurice!" She threw off the coverlet to reveal her husband's quaking frame. His long arms spread wide, fingers grasping at the mattress, he lay on his back shaking his head back and forth, moaning. His hair straggled across his face. Sweat glistened on his brow; his damp nightshirt clung to his chest and gaped at the neck, revealing sinews knotted as if he strained against bindings. The scar on his jawline showed white beneath his beard.

The rush of cold air made his breath catch. His eyelids fluttered. Tears streaked his temples.

"You are suffering a night terror, Jean-Maurice. Relax. You are safe at home." She touched his clammy forearm, ready to evade another wild swing.

He blinked. "Georgette. You are safe?"

Her jaw quivered with cold. "I am safe, as are you. That

was a dreadful dream. You yelled and thrashed and howled. Are you better now?"

"*Oui.*" His voice was quiet.

"Come and change into a fresh nightshirt, dearest. You are drenched in sweat." Teeth chattering, she stepped into his dressing room to find a clean garment. When she returned, he sat beside the hearth, stirring up the fire. The slump of his angular shoulders touched her heart. "Jean-Maurice?"

He glanced toward her, running his fingers through his tangled hair. "Thank you, but I shall change in my room. Come and warm yourself beside the fire until I return." She picked up a woolen shawl, wrapped it around her shoulders, and obeyed. Caramel sat up in his basket, blinking and yawning. After a quick survey of his humans, he tramped circles into his blankets and curled up to sleep once more.

When her husband returned and took the chair opposite hers, Georgette noticed his neatly brushed hair. "Did you wash? The water must have been icy."

"It was, but I could not subject you to a malodorous husband." A wry smile touched his lips before his gaze returned to the fire. He wore a fine silk banyan robe over his nightshirt, but his legs and feet were bare like hers. After three months, Georgette still found the informality of marriage intriguing.

Rising, she approached and knelt before him, looking up into his face. "Is it well with you, Jean-Maurice?"

He tugged off her nightcap and rested his cheek atop her head, placing his hands upon her shoulders. "Georgette, I love you so. Forgive me!"

"For loving me?"

"For being unworthy. If anything ever happened to you. . ." His voice trembled into silence. The grip on her shoulders tightened.

She reached between the lapels of his robe and laid her hand over his pounding heart. "You must learn to trust our

Lord with the future. He is the only one with power to save. Remember all we have read together about His redeeming love?"

He gripped her hand with his own and pressed it closer. His chilly skin warmed to her touch. After a long silence, he said quietly, *"Dieu ne peut pas m'aimer."*

Concentrating for a moment, Georgette interpreted "God cannot love me" and felt a shock. How could this be? From the depths of her spirit, she prayed for wisdom. "God loves everyone from the greatest saint to the lowest criminal. He loves you, Jean-Maurice. If I can love you, certainly God does."

He rose and stepped away to face a dark corner of the chamber, arms folded across his chest. "He knows all about me. You do not."

Fear of the anguish she had seen in his eyes haunted Georgette. Lady Forester's harsh warning rang in her ears. Had he been seeing other women even after vowing fidelity to her? She spoke calmly despite the pain in her chest. "God knows everyone's secret sins, and He promises to cleanse and forgive. In all our Bible reading, have we yet learned of a man whose sins were too great for God to forgive? Sometimes men refuse to repent; they scorn God's sovereignty and mock His gift of salvation. But that is their choice, not God's. Jesus came to die for all men. He associated with the worst sinners—murderers, thieves, and harlots."

"Why?"

"Because those people recognized their need of a Savior. They knew their unworthiness to approach God on their own."

He gave a grunt.

Was it a grunt of assent or of dissent?

Still kneeling before the empty chair, Georgette prayed. Had her words made any sense? She was groggy with sleep, and he was overwrought. She hoped God could use her feeble efforts.

He swung around and faced her. "Come to bed before you

fall ill." She accepted his outstretched hand and let him pull her up. Together they turned the featherbed and climbed into its billowing folds.

Jean-Maurice wrapped his arms around Georgette and gradually relaxed. Soon his deep breathing told her that he slept. An ache deeper than tears settled around her heart.

❧

"Miss Gigi." Yvonne laid a work-roughened hand on Georgette's shoulder. "You should get outside and take some fresh air. 'Twould do you good."

Georgette nodded, dragging her gaze from the coals on the kitchen hearth. "Perhaps I shall visit Francine." She closed the Bible in her lap and sighed.

Yvonne's skirts rustled against the wooden settle. "I should keep my place and mind my business, but I hate the sight of you and monsieur both moping about. Old Yvonne is good at listening to the woes of brides."

Georgette met Yvonne's sympathetic gaze and tried to smile. Tears sprang to her eyes; she dabbed at them with the corner of her apron. Yvonne sat down next to her. Georgette leaned on the older woman's sturdy shoulder, inhaling her scent of cinnamon and coffee. "Oh, Yvonne, I am such a fool."

Yvonne pressed her wrinkled cheek against Georgette's forehead and rocked gently. "*Ma fille,* tell Yvonne your folly."

"Mr. LaTournay—" A sob choked her for a moment. "He claimed to be a Christian. Only now, after months of marital happiness, do I learn that he does not accept God's forgiveness and salvation." The last words came out as a wail.

Yvonne remained quiet.

"His past troubles him, Yvonne, but he will not speak of it to me. He believes God cannot forgive him. And I have disobeyed God's command by marrying an unbeliever."

Yvonne nodded. "Noel and I shall pray twice as hard for the boy. You must know, Miss Gigi, that not all past sin and pain should be spoken of between husband and wife. Let him choose what he will share. And yet I agree with you that he must face his past and release it into God's hands."

"I am dreadfully confused. I should not have married Mr. LaTournay, and yet I love him so dearly that I cannot regret my error. I realize now that we had different understandings of the term 'Christian.' After being christened, he naturally considered himself a Christian. He did not know that I spoke of salvation through faith in Christ. But, Yvonne, had I known he was not a believer, I might have married him anyway. Is it sinful that I do not regret pledging myself to him for life?"

Yvonne stared into her eyes and gave her a gentle shake. "For shame, to waste time and tears so! God does not condemn us for the sins we might have committed had the situation been otherwise. He has enough to do forgiving us for the sins we actually commit. You erred through ignorance, and the deed is done. Now you must live with what is and obey what you know to be God's will. Do you think God would have you stop loving your husband?"

"No," Georgette whispered.

"Until Jean-Maurice met you, he rejected God altogether and his life was an empty shell. You are exactly what the boy needed—you have adored him, played with him, prayed with him, studied Scripture with him, and shared with him the depths of your heart. Your love is an essential piece to the puzzle of his questing soul. You have given him a taste of God's perfect love. Now we must trust that God will prevail in the end. Only He can complete your marriage. Only He can form Jean-Maurice into the godly man He intended him to be."

Georgette looked into Yvonne's eyes and felt hope for the first time in days. She hugged the elderly housekeeper and silently thanked God for providing her with wise counsel.

❧

Three days later, Jean-Maurice looked up from his evening

Scripture reading to announce: "I am leaving for New York City tomorrow."

Georgette's mouth fell open. Unwelcome thoughts flashed through her mind—Lady Forester, the Whig rebellion and its accompanying dangers, the Frog. *Has my husband tired of me so quickly?*

He laid the Bible on a side table and took a deep breath. "Information of an urgent nature impels this sudden journey. I would not leave you for a lesser cause."

"I shall go with you." She scarcely recognized her own voice.

He shook his head, though she recognized a hint of indecision. "The journey downriver in summer is difficult; in winter it is more arduous still. And you know of the unrest in the city." His eyes and jaw hardened. "Atrocities have been committed in the name of patriotism, and the innocent suffer. I cannot subject you to such danger, Georgette."

"What are you keeping from me?"

The slightest dilation of his pupils verified her suspicion. A dreadful certainty struck her. "It is my parents."

His shoulders stiffened. "How do you know?"

"Jean-Maurice, you must tell me!" She flung herself at his feet and clutched his knees. "What has happened? Are they alive?"

"They are alive." He cupped her face between his hands. "Georgette, do you hear? They are alive. Calm yourself, *épouse chérie.*"

Looking into his solemn eyes, she attempted to control her panic. "Did they not sail for England? Did the ship sink?" Her mind began to spin wild schemes. She must go with him to New York, no matter what the cost.

"The *Lily Fair* never sailed." He lifted her to sit upon his lap. The skirts of her bedgown engulfed him.

"The ship never sailed? But why?" Georgette twined her arms around his neck.

He remained unyielding in her embrace, and his voice stayed formal in tone. "I do not know why. Their passage was never refunded. A radical element in the city seized your father, then tarred and feathered him."

Georgette gasped as though she had received a blow to the stomach. "But why? And Mummy? Where have they lived? How have they survived these months?"

"I know not how they survived at first, but they currently reside at the Grenville estate on Long Island."

"So Marianne helped them. Now, of course, I must come with you," Georgette said. "Caramel will remain here with Yvonne and Noel. What? Why do you gaze at me with such trepidation and censure?" She smoothed the lines on his forehead with one finger and gave him a lingering kiss. His lips clung to hers as if he were helpless to resist. "Do you not wish to have me along?"

He closed his eyes and buried his head against her shoulder. "Do not make sport of me, Georgette. Your safety is my concern. If my desires alone were consulted, you and I would never part. This war escalates in scale and intensity. British troops are expected to invade New York soon, though no one knows when."

"I hope it is soon; then we shall all be safe." She felt tension in his neck muscles as her fingers stroked the smooth skin above his collar.

"Yet we cannot wait for that day, and should the invasion occur while we are there, our lives would certainly be endangered. Best to snatch your parents out of harm's way, a tactic easiest accomplished by one man alone. Before long the Hudson will close off with ice. If it happens too soon, we shall be obliged to travel overland."

She felt his hands roaming over her back, yet his mind seemed occupied with travel and tactics. Time to plant a suggestion. She spoke into his ear. "Jean-Maurice, you will make arrangements for our quick passage home while I care for my parents' immediate needs. Together we can accomplish more."

He kissed her neck. Maybe he was not completely preoccupied after all. Georgette lifted her chin and sighed her pleasure. "So I may come with you?"

His grasp tightened, and he kissed a trail up the side of her throat.

"Jean-Maurice?"

He lifted bemused eyes and a crooked smile. "I can deny you nothing, *ma petite.*"

❧

If anything, Mr. LaTournay had understated the misery of winter travel. Great chunks of ice floated alongside the boats traversing the river, and a contrary breeze impeded progress while freezing the passengers' faces. Georgette huddled in the stern beneath layers of oilcloth, blankets, and cloaks. It must be late afternoon, but the sleety weather and gray gloom had changed little since early-morning hours.

A corner of her shelter lifted. Her husband squatted before her. "Georgette, we shall arrive on Manhattan Island in approximately two hours. There we must hire horses to carry us to the ferry landing. I know not what political climate we shall find in the city, but 'twould profit us to say nothing to anyone about our business."

She nodded. Though she would have liked to complain about her frozen extremities and the complete lack of privacy, coming along on this trip had, after all, been her idea. Mr. LaTournay seemed to read her mind. His eyes crinkled above the muffler wrapped over his mouth and nose. His cheeks were cherry red from the whipping wind and blowing snow. Dancing wisps of dark hair caught in his brows and draped over his nose. He lifted his three-cornered hat, brushed back the hair with one hand, and replaced the hat. "Solid ground will come as a treat, eh?"

Georgette nodded. "And a hotel." With a hot bath, if at all possible.

"I shall try to find us lodging at the boardinghouse."

She looked at his chapped hands clad in fingerless gloves. He must be as uncomfortable as she, yet he seemed accustomed to a harsh environment. Georgette felt weak and useless. No wonder he had not wished to bring her along. She was nothing but trouble for him.

"Might there be difficulty in renting a room for the night?"

He shifted position, setting one knee down. "The proprietor might have fled the city by now. Word is that many citizens have emigrated to other cities or colonies."

Georgette nodded mutely.

He reached beneath the oilcloth to touch her face with his icy fingers. "I shall find lodging for you, *ma belle épouse,* never fear. You have been most courageous." He winked one red-rimmed eye and dropped her cover back into place.

A moment later, she heard him speaking to one of the boatmen in rapid-fire French. These men seemed to know him well. Everyone seemed to know Mr. LaTournay, she realized with irritation. Often she sensed, with a surge of jealousy, that other people knew him better than she did. She had given herself to him completely; why must he be so tight-lipped and reserved? Even during their most private moments, she sensed times when he checked himself, as if he feared revealing too much of his soul.

Jean-Maurice desired her; Georgette held no doubts in that regard. He expressed sincere admiration and gratitude, and his eyes communicated ardor more eloquently than his tongue. She felt more beautiful than ever before in her life, and perhaps she should have been content. Yet she wanted more.

Whenever her husband spoke to her tenderly in French, her heart responded with an intensity that astonished her. Only one other man had ever affected her so—a man she endeavored to forget. It could not be the French accent alone, for none of the many Frenchmen she had met while living in Paris had caused such havoc to her emotions.

Occasionally she pondered the similarities between Jean-Maurice and her mysterious hero. Both men were French, both tall and vigorous, both kind and considerate. She knew the Frog to be a man of honor, despite his absurd appellation and traitorous activities. Notwithstanding his cynical, teasing behavior at their first meeting, he had treated her with respect. Even while declaring his devotion at their subsequent meetings, not once had he disgusted her with a suggestion of immorality.

Was the Frog still alive? Would he see her enter the city and find a way to contact her? Guilt swept over Georgette even as she allowed the treacherous thoughts.

❧

They took lodgings that night at Hull's Tavern. After making sure she would have the bath she craved, her husband donned his coat and cloak. "I must make arrangements for tomorrow and inquiries about your parents, Georgette. You will be safe here in the room. I shall return in time to bathe before supper."

"Take care," she warned.

His weather-burned face creased into a smile. "Always."

True to his word, he reappeared while Georgette combed out her hair beside the fire. "The water is tepid," she said. "We can request a kettle of hot water."

"I have already done so." He opened the door in response to a knock, and a boy carrying a steaming kettle entered. Without a word, the boy emptied the pot into the tub. Mr. LaTournay pressed a coin into his hand and closed the door behind him.

The room contained no privacy screen. Georgette watched her husband remove his cravat and waistcoat. Embarrassed, she averted her gaze until he submerged himself in the tub. Blowing and sputtering, he surfaced, hair and beard dripping. "Not quite hot enough but far warmer than the Hudson," he said. "Please hand me the scrub brush and soap."

Georgette obliged. Dark hair lay plastered on his exposed knees, forearms, and chest. His wet shoulders reflected the firelight as he applied the scrub brush to his sinewy back. He grinned up at her. "The last woman who watched me bathe was my mother."

Heat suffused her face. Turning to the mirror, she began to pin up her still-damp hair but could not avoid hearing his chuckle.

"I fear my gown is out of style."

"The trade ships from England did not arrive here in October, so everyone in the city is wearing last year's fashions." Splashes and thumps told her when he climbed out of the tub. She could not resist sneaking a peek in the mirror while he dressed. His twinkling dark eyes met her gaze as he tightened the drawstring of his drawers.

Although she wanted to be offended or shocked, Georgette found herself smiling. Judging by his reaction, it was not a bad thing that she found him good to look upon. "Woman, you are a distraction," he growled. Instead of pulling on his shirt, he approached her to claim a kiss.

Nestled in his arms, Georgette inhaled the fragrance of his clean skin. "I am glad I came with you."

"At the moment, I, too, am thankful. I hope I may remain so." He stepped back. "We must make haste if we are to dine tonight."

Georgette reluctantly let him finish dressing.

❧

Moonlight streamed through a window, unimpeded by the wisp of curtain. Although the bed was clean and vermin-free, Georgette could not sleep. Voices from the taproom below were just loud enough to annoy without allowing her to distinguish one word from another. Her supper of fried ham and beans was not setting well.

Her husband's deep breathing told Georgette that he slept. Shivering despite layers of blankets, she snuggled up against his broad back and thought wistfully of the luxurious featherbeds back home. He rolled over to embrace her, encroaching on much of her bed space. The price of warmth. Georgette rested her cheek against his chest and let the strong beat of his heart soothe her.

Just as her mind drifted into sleep, a sharper beat awakened her. Mr. LaTournay sat up and placed a restraining hand on Georgette when she opened her mouth to inquire. The rapping sounded again.

With astonishing suddenness and silence, Mr. LaTournay positioned himself beside the chamber door. "Who is there?"

"Pringle. I need to talk to you."

"One moment." He hauled on his breeches as he spoke. His nightshirt gleamed white as it floated to the floor. Georgette lost sight of him in the shadows but heard evidence of his preparation. He suddenly loomed over her. "Never fear. I'll not be long."

She clung to him for an instant, returned his kiss, and released him. The door opened, admitting a louder volume of taproom clamor, then closed. Its latch clicked into place.

As soon as he was gone, Georgette thought of a dozen questions to ask.

twelve

But if ye will not do so, behold, ye have sinned against the LORD: and be sure your sin will find you out.
NUMBERS 32:23

"You were in bed?" Pringle inquired as he led the way downstairs. "At this hour? My, how marriage has countrified you, LaTournay."

LaTournay glanced into the small taproom in passing. "Does not the Provincial Congress regulate the closing hour of taverns as it polices everything else in town?"

Pringle gave an appreciative snort as he hauled on his overcoat. "I imagine the taproom currently contains an associator or two. Rules are made to be broken only by those who enforce them."

LaTournay observed while his friend hunched in the tavern doorway and scanned the street. "Eyes are always watching," Pringle said. "You can have no idea what these past months have been. Daily we hope and pray that Governor Tryon will succeed in convincing General Howe to make New York his center of operations."

Thinking of his warm bed, LaTournay reluctantly followed Pringle. For all his efforts, Pringle moved with the finesse of a rolling boulder. The heels of his shoes tapped on the cobblestones, and he could not seem to restrain a stream of conversation. "The associators have detained me more than once, insisting that I take an oath of allegiance. I tell them I already signed and swore it once and do not intend to do so again."

"It does seem an ineffective measure—coerced fealty. You say you did swear it once?"

"Only to remove suspicion from myself. An informant is useless when he is suspected."

The men turned east on Crown Street. A blast of winter wind struck, slicing through layers of clothing. LaTournay drew his cloak together at the neck and hunched his shoulders. "So you still spy for the army?" he asked as they approached the docks.

"I work for Governor Tryon now. Since he moved his office aboard the *Duchess of Gordon,* he needs eyes and ears in town. I move with the stealth and quickness of a panther. That is my code name—the Panther."

"Selecting one's own alias offers distinct advantages." LaTournay dragged one hand down over his mouth and beard in an effort to keep a straight face.

Diverse structures lined the street, from rickety shops surrounded by heaps of refuse to brick townhouses with manicured gardens. The scent of rotting fish blended with wood smoke and sea salt. Deep grunts and strident squeals divulged the presence of nocturnal garbage looters. LaTournay hoped the beasts were of a peaceable nature. Swine ranged among his least favored of God's creation.

"Why did Governor Tryon move to a ship?" he asked.

"He caught wind of a plot to kidnap him," Pringle replied. "Although the Provincial Congress swears it intended no such scheme, who can place credence in the assurances of traitors?"

"Who, indeed?"

Pringle stopped him suddenly. "We are followed. Come." He ducked behind the short hedge lining a town house's garden.

LaTournay crouched beside his friend. "Who could it be, do you think? An associator?" He and Pringle were being shadowed, LaTournay knew, but the real trackers would not so carelessly betray their presence.

Pringle made a hacking motion to halt the questions. Hooves clacked on the cobblestones, and two hogs trotted past, ears flopping.

Pringle let out his breath as the two men stood upright. "False alarm this time. LaTournay, you disappoint me. You must learn to practice caution if you're to survive in this city more than a day. I depend upon you to help organize our Tories into troops that should impress even Howe. You may know little about military matters, but your voice and demeanor will inspire confidence, which I confess is a trait sadly lacking at present."

LaTournay followed Pringle back to the walkway. "I, organize troops? Pringle, you flatter me."

"I have something to show you. Come."

"I cannot become involved."

Pringle shook his head. "You think so now, but not when you have seen and heard all."

Gripping his friend's arm, LaTournay tugged him to a halt. "Listen. My wife awaits my return. I cannot stay out long. What is so urgent that you drag me from my bed into the frigid night?"

"Your sad fate motivates me. I have a long and tragic tale to relate. Will you not come with me to Queens? A boat awaits us at the landing."

LaTournay paused before answering. "Not tonight. My plans take me there tomorrow. To Grenville's estate in Queens County, where my wife's relations bide until our coming."

Pringle laughed aloud. "But of course! Better still to reveal all with the wench present. Your plan could scarcely be improved upon. Very well. I shall meet you there." Exuberant as ever, he prepared to bound away.

LaTournay caught his arm again. "Do not refer to my wife in disrespectful terms. Are you married?"

"Married?"

"To Miss Grenville. I had understood that nuptials were forthcoming."

Pringle laughed. "Never if I can help it."

"Have you yet apprehended the Toad?"

A pause. "I assume you speak of the spy I call the Frog."

"Frog, toad, it matters little." LaTournay waved it off.

"We have not apprehended him as yet, but I expect to shortly. We shall soon have the proper gig with which to snare frogs. I anticipate skewering this particular animal and frying its legs in butter."

"I pity the unwary creature you capture, Pringle. Are you not taking this contention too personally? With what 'gig' do you expect to entrap this frog?"

"That you shall discover on the morrow, my friend—to your sorrow, I fear." Pringle's laugh held little mirth. "I am a poet, you see, as well as a prophet. We shall lure this cuckolding frog from out of his concealing fog."

❧

Georgette stiffened when the chamber door creaked open. She gripped her bedclothes beneath her chin.

"It is I; never fear."

At the sound of her husband's voice, she felt as limp as overcooked cabbage. "Where have you been?"

"Let me join you before I answer that question." Sounds of rustling fabric followed. His silhouette passed the window moments before he climbed into bed beside her.

"Ooh!" she gasped as his icy arms and legs pressed against hers. His entire body shivered. She let him pull her close and soak in her warmth. "Now tell me."

"Pringle wished to take me to Long Island."

"Tonight?"

"I explained our plan to travel there tomorrow."

"I assume he found that plan satisfactory." Georgette rubbed her husband's frozen forearms. "So he dragged you out into the cold night for no good reason. I do not comprehend your continuing friendship with that man, Jean-Maurice. He cannot be a good influence. Do you wish to return to your old lifestyle?" The question that had plagued her for days popped out, taking her by surprise.

"My old lifestyle?"

"The immoral lifestyle of an unmarried man. I am well aware of your reputation. My mother says a woman should never speak of such things or even acknowledge awareness of her husband's foibles, but I cannot imagine practicing deceit on that scale."

"On what scale can you imagine practicing deceit?"

"None whatever! A husband and wife should be honest with one another." She sat up and turned to confront him, although darkness negated the effect of her stare. "Do you wish to be unfaithful to me?"

He gave an incredulous huff. "You can even ask this? Georgette, I desire no woman but you, ever." Anger tinged his voice.

She dared not yet relax in relief. "I find it necessary to ask for two reasons. One, because of your past indiscretions. Two, because I know that you hide much of your heart and mind from me."

"I hide none of my heart from you. I love you. I have never loved another woman. For reasons I cannot reveal, I allowed people to believe that Lady Forester and I were romantically linked. The fabrication was hers; I simply neglected to repudiate it, and people chose to believe the lie. Tales of my liaisons with additional women are entirely fictitious. Others of God's commandments I confess I have broken, but the seventh remains sacrosanct."

"Is this true?"

"Ask me again in daylight if you doubt. I can no longer maintain the charade before my wife, come what may."

He sounded defiant. Something about the confession seemed odd, but Georgette was too tired to ponder the matter. "I believe you. Oh, Jean-Maurice, I love you so much! It hurt terribly to think that you would ever tire of me and seek another woman. My mother told me to expect it."

"Your mother does not know me." He tightened his grip

around her waist, pulling her down. Georgette's tears dampened his nightshirt as she clung to him. "Are you crying?" he asked.

"Because I am happy," she confessed. He stroked her head, dislodging her nightcap. She felt a deep sigh expand his chest.

❧

Snow dusted the gloves holding the reins—Georgette could not think of those numb hands as hers. The roached mane of her roan horse held an extra frost, though the snow melted on contact with the beast's sweating shoulders. To her befuddled brain, the animal appeared to breathe like a dragon—twin jets of smoke emerged from its nostrils.

Georgette ached in every bone and muscle. A sleepless night followed by a day of riding, all coming at the end of a most uncomfortable journey—she could hardly remain upright in the sidesaddle.

"Not long now," Jean-Maurice encouraged her.

"How many times have you visited Grenville Grange?" she asked, nudging her horse alongside her husband's.

"Once or twice. Beautiful countryside here." He scanned the rolling farmland. "Pleasant villages, scenic vistas."

Georgette squinted at her surroundings. Even with its frosted, winter-bare trees and fields, the island held a lush beauty. "I like our home better. I hope my father is well enough to travel, for I wish to remain not a day longer than necessary. How I long for our cozy fireside and snug featherbeds!" The scarf she had wrapped around her nose and mouth felt stiff with the frozen condensation of her breath.

Jean-Maurice reached across to squeeze her hand. The pressure hurt, but at least she knew her extremities were still alive. "I, too." He winked at her, and his eyes crinkled above his knitted muffler.

Grenville Grange sat back from the main road, surrounded by a sweep of snowy turf. Towering trees framed its black, gabled roofline. Multiple outbuildings indicated Grenville's prosperity.

The powdery snow had not yet accumulated on the circular drive. Mr. LaTournay tied his horse to a ring before lifting Georgette from the sidesaddle. Her right leg gave way as soon as it touched the ground. "I cannot bear weight on it," she groaned, clutching her husband's forearm.

"The feeling will soon return." He walked her slowly in a circle. The skirts of her riding habit swept frost from the lawn.

Two young black men approached to take the horses. When Mr. LaTournay thanked them, they gave him wary looks of surprise and said nothing.

"Slaves," he said flatly. "And Grenville claims to be a Christian."

While Georgette's thoughts flurried, a door clicked open behind them. "Gigi! Is it really you?"

Turning, Georgette laughed. "I wish I could say yes, but at the moment I am uncertain even of my own identity."

"Mr. Pringle told us you were coming—he returned this morning—but Papa thought this weather would delay your arrival. I imagine the ferry ride was miserable." Marianne picked up her skirts and stepped over muddy ruts to greet her friend. After bestowing a kiss upon Georgette's cheek, she stood back to look her up and down. "Come in and warm yourselves. It is also good to see you again, Mr. LaTournay."

"My pleasure, Miss Grenville." He bowed.

"Your parents will be delighted to see you, Gigi. Your father is still ailing, but his color is better and his hair begins to grow back." Marianne gripped Georgette's hand and led her inside. Mr. LaTournay followed.

"A servant is bringing our things, although we do not expect to remain long," Georgette said. "We must hurry home, for the Hudson will soon be impossible to navigate."

Marianne said nothing, but her expression gave Georgette an uneasy twinge. She escorted them into a large sitting room with a roaring fire upon the hearth. Three shawl-wrapped figures huddled in chairs around the hearth. "Mother? Mr. and Mrs. Talbot? Gigi and Mr. LaTournay are here."

Georgette's mother dropped her knitting and leaped up to greet her. Georgette clung to her, tears streaming down her cheeks. "Mummy, I thought never to see you again!"

"Darling girl, you look wonderful! So rosy and elegant. You are happy?"

"I could not be more so," Georgette said. "Mr. LaTournay is good to me, and our home is lovely. We plan to take you there. Papa should recover quickly in the fresh country air." She cast an apprehensive glance at her father, who had not yet lifted his gaze from the fire.

"And dear Mr. LaTournay." Her mother extended a hand to her son-in-law and accepted his dutiful kiss.

"Welcome to our home, Georgette." Marianne's mother spoke stiffly. "Welcome, Mr. LaTournay," she added with more warmth. "I shall retire at present to give you privacy, but we shall meet at dinner. Would you like chocolate brought to your chambers?"

"Yes, thank you, Mrs. Grenville. We are eternally indebted for your provision of a haven for my parents during their time of need." Georgette took the woman's offered hand and curtsied. Her legs cramped, but she managed to rise without grimacing. Mrs. Grenville swept from the room, chin held high.

"Let me show you to your chambers so you can freshen up." Marianne sounded too bright and cheery.

"Hello, Father," Georgette said. "I hope you are feeling better."

Her father gave her a cursory glance and focused on her husband. "You heard what they did to me?" He described his tormentors in profane terms. The three ladies exchanged uncomfortable glances.

"We were deeply disturbed to hear of it," Mr. LaTournay said. "Only the lowest individuals would perpetrate such abuse upon their fellow man. No excuse can be tendered for this dishonorable offense. If you please, I shall join you here by the fire so that you may relate details of the experience without further distressing the ladies."

"Come then." Her father indicated an empty chair.

Mr. LaTournay first took Georgette's elbow and bent to speak quietly. "Go ahead; enjoy your time with Marianne. Your father needs to vent his outrage to someone other than ladies."

Although her father's rebuff hurt, Georgette tried to feel sympathy. "He has endured great pain and indignity," she whispered. "Thank you."

A faint smile softened his expression, and he gave her arm a gentle squeeze.

Marianne chattered as she led the way up two flights of stairs. "I am sorry we have only third-floor chambers left for you and Mr. LaTournay, but your parents occupy our best guest rooms. You have windows overlooking our little valley, and the rooms should be warm, since I ordered Trixie to light fires in them this morning."

"I am certain we shall be comfortable. I cannot begin to express my gratitude to your family, Marianne. What would my parents have done without your care?" Georgette's legs wobbled as she neared the third-floor landing. "Exactly how long have they been here?"

"Papa found them in late October. Their ship put them off and sailed to Jamaica."

"Without refunding their passage. Is that not criminal? Can we not report this to the shipping company and receive their refund?"

Marianne pushed open a door near the end of the upper hallway. "Here is your chamber. Mr. LaTournay's is adjoining." She stepped inside before responding to Georgette's question. "Gigi, your father says they did not refund the passage, but your mother says otherwise. They lived on the money until my father found them. They might have purchased passage on another ship. . . ."

"Except that my father gambled much of it away first, I imagine." Georgette completed the sentence with a sigh. "This is a fine room." She smoothed the counterpane on a large four-poster bed.

"Gigi, are you happily married? Please tell me the truth." Marianne looked grave. "Mr. Pringle has told me terrible things. . . ."

"I am content, Marianne. My husband is good to me, and we love each other. We have our disagreements, naturally, and there is much I still must learn about him, but on the whole I would say we are well matched. What can Mr. Pringle have said that is so terrible?" Georgette untied her bonnet and dropped it upon the bed. Until her trunk arrived, she would have to remain in her riding habit.

"I am thankful to hear it," Marianne said. She strolled about the small room, tugging at the curtain, poking the fire, straightening a candlestick. "Ah, here is Trixie with your chocolate." Marianne relieved the slave woman of the tray. "You may go."

Trixie bowed her turbaned head and slipped into the hall. Georgette could not help comparing her with effervescent Yvonne.

Marianne poured a cup of the steaming beverage. "Do you take sugar?"

"Two spoonfuls, please. When is your wedding date?" Georgette asked as she accepted the cup, cradling its warmth in her hands.

"We have set no date. I am uncertain the wedding will ever take place, Gigi. Mr. Pringle is busy with prepar—" She broke off, gave Georgette a nervous glance, and continued. "He is so busy these days with business that we never speak of love." Her blue eyes held deep sadness.

"I am sorry." Georgette did not know what to say.

Marianne hurried to the door. "Dinner is served at six; we dine early in the country." She paused. "Oh, Gigi, had I not promised secrecy, I would warn you of what is to come. Your father is so angry—yet I am certain it cannot be true. No, do not importune me to tell you, for I cannot. Pray for wisdom and courage, my dearest Gigi. I shall be praying for you."

She slipped into the hallway, leaving Georgette to wrack her brain for an explanation.

❧

Les Pringle bounded in during the meat course, apologizing profusely as he seated himself at the table. He had not even bothered to change out of his riding clothes. "An eventful, auspicious day. Good evening to you all. Ah, Mrs. LaTournay."

He rose from his seat again and approached Georgette to bow. "Welcome to Grenville Grange. As you see, we have given your worthy parents the best of care. I had not the pleasure of congratulating you upon your marriage before Mr. LaTournay swept you off north. Allow me now to express my sincere wish that your future will hold the amount of happiness you deserve." He kissed her hand with moist lips. The look in his eyes and the tone of his voice disturbed Georgette.

When Pringle returned to his seat, Georgette glanced across the table at her husband. Mr. LaTournay looked as baffled as she felt. Forks and knives rattled against porcelain dishes. Mr. Grenville sent the veal back to the kitchen, complaining that it was overcooked. The pungent aromas of heavily spiced mutton and broiled oysters competed for precedence. Georgette picked at her vegetables, longing for the moment she and her husband could retire for the night. A wave of homesickness struck her.

Dinner conversation revolved around farming and the shipping business. Mr. Pringle spoke with brilliance and animation, drawing the ladies into the discussion whenever possible. Mr. and Mrs. Grenville seemed enamored of him, but Georgette noticed a decided coolness on Marianne's part. She could not help feeling relieved. Marianne must finally have seen through the man's handsome mask to the scoundrel he truly was.

During the sweetmeat and cheese course, Pringle raised a hand to draw attention to himself. "Before another moment passes, we must clear the air and place all our cards upon the table."

A hush followed the announcement. Pringle's face expressed unaccustomed dignity and remorse. "It grieves me to cause pain to anyone, let alone to a good friend, but it must be done for the good of all. Mr. LaTournay, I have the grim obligation of informing you that your wife is untrue. While pledged to you, she entertained and gave comfort to another man. She is traitor both to you and to England."

Georgette choked on a bite of almond tart, coughed into her napkin, and took a quick sip of perry. The sparkling pear juice burned in her stomach.

In the deathly silence following her coughing attack, Mr. LaTournay turned to Georgette. "Is this true?" His eyes held a watchful calm.

"I–I—yes, I did see another man, but only to tell him that I could no longer receive him." Her tired mind spun in circles of conjecture. "If I betrayed England in any way, it was unwittingly done."

Pringle tossed a few raisins into his mouth and emitted a sharp laugh, talking while he chewed. "The man must have been slow to understand, for you saw him several times last summer. Is it not true that your dog was a gift from this man and that you once entertained him while clad only in your nightclothes?"

Heat flooded Georgette's face. "No! I mean, well, yes, but not in the way you imply. He came into the garden one night, and I ran down to tell him he must leave."

"And did you or did you not warn this man, a spy and traitor known as the Frog, that we Loyalists had laid a trap for him?"

Pringle's voice rang through the room. "Hardly an 'unwitting' treachery."

Georgette's gaze skittered across the other accusing faces to focus upon her husband's dark eyes. They seemed empty, devoid of expression, as if he were a stranger she had never met and would never know. "Jean-Maurice, you must believe that I have never been unfaithful to you! This man had been kind to me; I could not allow him to be captured without warning him of the plot."

Mr. LaTournay looked at Pringle. "How do you know these things?"

Pringle snapped his fingers at a footman. "Bring in the woman called Biddy."

"Biddy!" Georgette breathed the name aloud.

The tiny woman entered, wide-eyed and apologetic. "Missy Georgette, I never would have told if not for the way that Frog has hurt our soldiers. Please forgive me for spying on you, missy!"

"Tell these people what you told me, Biddy," Pringle demanded. "How did Mrs. LaTournay react when you brought her the notes from this Frog spy?"

"Forgive me, missy—but she smiled so bright it seemed like the stars lit in her eyes. I said to myself that the lady must be in love to react so. And the dog, he represented that lover to her, no doubt in my mind. When that Frog first brought the puppy, she showed herself at the window in her chemise. Shocked, I was, and thinking she must have known this cloaked man before."

"No! I never did." Georgette gasped for breath, feeling smothered.

Mr. LaTournay slid back his chair and rose. "You deliberately aided a Whig spy? You entertained another man at night? That dog you treasure was a gift from this Frog?" Never before had he addressed Georgette in such lifeless tones. "And you accuse me of keeping secrets."

Turning to his stunned host and hostess, he said, "Please excuse me. I must have time to think. I shall take a room in a nearby town." After a bow to the room in general, he made a quick exit.

Georgette felt her heart shatter into jagged shards.

thirteen

Then said Jesus unto the twelve, "Will ye also go away?"
JOHN 6:67

"How can I do this thing?" Georgette pleaded. "I am no siren to lure a man to his capture or death!" She pushed the paper aside and turned away from the writing desk. Scattered about the parlor, the Grenvilles and the Talbots watched the proceedings in condemning silence. Georgette felt new sympathy for martyrs of the Inquisition.

"You care more about this traitorous spy than about your husband," Pringle accused. "I warned LaTournay, but he refused to listen."

"Love for my husband does not mean I will sign the death warrant of another man. Do you think me a heartless monster?"

"Yes, in fact, I do." Pringle grinned. "Write the note, woman, before I find it expedient to take more forceful measures." He slapped his gloves against his thigh.

"Mr. Pringle, you would not strike Gigi," Marianne said, her voice shaking.

"I would strike a woman only if provoked. My patience wears thin." His smile did not reach his gleaming blue eyes. "This woman deserves only contempt and harsh treatment until she makes restitution for her breach of faith. I shall keep constant watch upon her while she remains in this house."

"Mr. LaTournay demands this of me?" Georgette picked up the quill and studied its point. "That I play false to a friend?"

"He expects this and much more before he will again welcome you into his home and affections. A man once betrayed will not easily be fooled again."

Thoughts rambled through Georgette's mind as she toyed with the goose quill. Recently Jean-Maurice had been pondering God's forgiveness; she knew because she had seen him deep in study of Scripture when he believed himself observed by no one. Had her apparent perfidy soured his perception of Jesus Christ? Had her weakness for romance destroyed her husband's hope for salvation?

She did not want or need any lover besides Jean-Maurice. Even so, her heart quailed at the prospect of bringing harm to her secret friend. Would the Frog come to her if summoned? Perhaps he would be out of town. Perhaps he had found another love and would scorn an invitation from a married woman. He might have forgotten her by now. Georgette could only hope.

Dipping her quill into the ink, she penned a short plea for aid. "I do not know how it will be delivered," she remarked after sealing it with a few drops of bayberry candle wax. "One can hardly address a missive to a frog."

"Leave that to me." Pringle snatched the note from her hand. "You should not have sealed it until I read it." He broke the seal and scanned her note, nodding in approval. "The very thing. Seal it again. I shall send a courier to town this night. Within two days we shall have this Frog in hand, I swear it!"

Later, despite a fire on the hearth and Trixie's application of a warming pan between her sheets, Georgette felt chilled to the bone. She wept alone in the four-poster bed. Inarticulate prayers poured from her heart, a longing for forgiveness and a return to love. "I shall confess all, if he will but grant me opportunity. Dear Lord, only You can bring good out of this terrible evil. Please protect the Frog, and please bring my husband back to me."

An icy draft awakened her during the night. Blinking away sleep, she rolled over, pulled aside the bed curtains, and stared at the window, visible as a pale smudge in the darkness of her chamber. As coals flared weakly on the hearth, Georgette beheld white draperies sweeping into the room like grasping ghostly arms. Someone or something had opened the window.

She sat up. "Who is there?" The window clicked shut, and frigid silence returned.

Georgette thought her heart might batter its way through her ribs. Dread and cold brought on a wave of nausea. Her limbs trembled uncontrollably, and her teeth chattered.

A black shadow tossed a faggot into the coals. A flame burst forth to lick at the bundle of dry sticks. The sight of a swirling cloak and gleaming boots brought Georgette intense relief—her midnight visitor was human, not goblin. "Frog?" she whispered.

"*Bon nuit, ma petite grenouille.* Pleased am I that you do not scream at sight of me." He approached the bed as silently as he had entered the room, speaking just above a whisper.

Georgette clutched her coverlet beneath her chin. "How. . . ? Why are you here? You cannot already have received the note. If you are found in my chamber, your life will be forfeit and mine forever ruined."

He pushed the bed curtain fully open. "I come on an errand of mercy, *ma belle.*" Backlit by the crackling fire, he made an impressive figure. "I cannot leave you in ignorance even one more hour, though it cost me everything. I come to confess." He knelt beside the bed and caught her hand. Rough leather gloves abraded her fingers as she twisted them in his grasp. His other hand reached to cup the back of her head.

"No!" She panicked. "You must leave! This is not right."

He shifted upward to sit on the edge of the bed frame. "Hush, *ma épouse chérie,* trust me. This is very right." He hauled her into his lap and cradled her close. A frosty beard brushed her cheek, and melting snow dampened her night-shift. He smelled of wet horse, fresh air, and coffee. His cool lips pressed against hers, warming rapidly at her response.

Understanding broke over Georgette like an avalanche, and she clutched her husband's broad shoulders in a fever of excitement. He kissed her cheeks, her neck, murmuring endearments in French.

She touched his beloved features. "Jean-Maurice, you still love me? I do not understand—you—are you the Frog?"

"Always I shall love you, Georgette. This Frog and I are one and the same, although the name I did not choose." His cold nose pressed into her neck. "You betrayed me with myself, beguiling woman that you are."

She struggled in protest. "I never betrayed you! Recall how I sent you away." She paused, frowning. "Why did you deceive me so? Jean-Maurice, I have been in agony this day, thinking you no longer cared for me!"

He groaned softly. "That is why I have risked all to come this night. Tomorrow, if you love your husband, you must play the actress and feign a broken heart."

"But you are a traitor to England?" Georgette began to apprehend the implications of his deception.

A quiet knock at the chamber door stunned them both to silence. "Georgette?"

Georgette flung herself at the door and opened it a tiny crack, jamming her foot at its base to keep it from opening wider. "Yes, Mother?"

A candle's flame lighted her mother's features. She blinked in evident surprise at Georgette's vigorous response. "Are you well? I heard movement; our chamber is beneath yours. Would you like me to sit with you tonight?"

"I want to be left alone," Georgette answered in her best petulant tone. "My life is ruined, and I wish to see no one. Go away." She closed the door.

"Very well, dearest. Despite all you have done, I love you."

Georgette leaned her forehead against the door. "I love you, too, Mummy." She assuaged her guilt by determining to be extra kind to her mother in the morning.

Turning, she scanned the room. Had she dreamed Jean-Maurice's appearance? Shivering, she hurried to climb back into bed and nearly screamed when her hand touched flesh. "Surprise," a deep voice said.

"Your boots," she whispered, imagining spurs shredding the linen sheets.

"*Maman* taught me never to wear shoes in bed. Come join me." When he rolled to his back and reached for her, she realized that he lay crosswise on the bed with his feet hanging off the far side.

"Can you stay awhile?" She climbed in beside him, wrapped her arms around his body, and rested her head upon his buckskin-fringed shirtfront. He embraced her gently.

"*Quel dommage!* How I wish it could be so." His beard tickled her forehead as he spoke.

"Mr. Pringle said he would have me watched," Georgette whispered. "Are you certain no one saw you enter my window? How did you climb up here? The roof is steep and high!"

"The Frog is part squirrel, and the trees are close." He caressed her back. "Pringle is unaware that Grenville's slaves are friendly with my servant Pierre Dimieux. They watched me enter and they keep guard."

"Pierre—Yvonne's son." Georgette remembered the handsome young hostler.

"And Noel's son. My closest friend since childhood, my faithful bodyguard, and the finest woodsman I know. Georgette, I request you to play the brokenhearted woman tomorrow and display strong feeling for the Frog. My mission depends upon you. Do you trust me?" He caught her face between his hands.

Although doubts crowded into her thoughts, Georgette nodded. "I shall do whatever you say, Jean-Maurice. But I am no actress. How can I do this?"

"Imagine how you would behave if this Frog were your lover and you had betrayed him to his doom." Jean-Maurice sat up, cradled her in his arms, and kissed her. "Pray for guidance and pray for me, *ma petite grenouille.*"

"Always. I love you." She reached to touch his back as he scooted off the far side of the bed. Despite the boots, his tread on the floorboards was nearly inaudible. He lifted the window sash and slipped outside with startling suddenness. Georgette rushed to the window and peered through the frosted glass, but he might have taken flight for all the evidence of him visible below.

❧

The following day seemed an eternity. Georgette helped her mother untangle yarns and knitted part of a sock. Her mind kept wandering, and she unraveled at least three socks' worth of work before ending up with less than one finished product. Her father still had not addressed her, and she feared he never would. Her mother chatted nervously, avoiding the subject that weighed heaviest on all minds.

During the noon meal, her father leveled his leaden gaze and his fork at Georgette. "If not for your stupidity, LaTournay would have purchased passage to England for your mother and me by now. You had better make this right. Do not expect us to take you in if LaTournay throws you out."

Georgette stared in disbelief at this new evidence of her father's disregard for the feelings of others. The Grenvilles attempted to brush over the awkward moment, but Georgette saw her mother's hands shaking as she buttered her bread. Georgette wished she could offer her mother sanctuary at Haven Farm. Her appreciation for Mr. LaTournay's kindness increased with each passing day.

As Georgette entered the drawing room shortly before dinner, a maid brought her a note: *Come to the apple orchard at midnight.* A drawing that must be intended as a frog served as signature.

A hand reached from behind Georgette and snatched the paper out of her fingers. Pringle scanned it. "Ah, he is drawn as a moth to the flame." He scrutinized Georgette. "I never understood why LaTournay fell for you, although you do have your. . .assets." He lifted a brow. "This Frog must share LaTournay's weakness."

She drew her shawl closer around her shoulders and turned away from his crude gaze.

Paper crackled. "The apple orchard at midnight." Mr. Pringle sounded displeased. "Difficult to conceal men there, but we shall have to contrive a way. If you give this spy so much as a hint of warning, I shall shoot you down like a. . .a frog. It is fitting that a frog should find you appealing. One large mouth must attract another."

"Mr. Pringle!" Marianne stepped into the room, her face crimson. "How cruel! You are no gentleman to speak so to a lady."

Chagrin flitted across his chiseled features. "This is no lady. She is a spy, Marianne—a spy who betrayed her husband and her country. Such a woman deserves no courtesy."

Georgette produced a sob and a few tears. Burying her face in her hands, she rushed out of the room and upstairs, pausing to catch her breath on the first landing. To her surprise, Marianne had followed her.

"Darling Gigi! How your heart must be breaking!" Marianne led the way into her own drawing room and closed the door.

Georgette sighed. "Marianne, why must life be so confusing? Why does God allow certain prayers to remain unanswered?"

"He answers every prayer, Gigi, but sometimes His answer is 'no' or 'wait.' From our limited perspective, these prayers appear unanswered. Do you love this Frog so much? I thought you loved Mr. LaTournay."

"But I do! Oh, Marianne, I cannot explain."

Marianne sat on a settee and patted the seat. "Is the Frog handsome?" she asked as Georgette sat down.

A twinge of jealousy pinched Georgette. Then she nearly

laughed aloud at her own folly. "His face is always concealed. He is a tall, active man with a beautiful voice. He speaks of love to me in French."

In French. How blind she was! Georgette decided that had she been married to Jean-Maurice when first she met the Frog, he would not have deceived her so easily. He would not have deceived her at all.

"I detect tenderness for him in your voice." Marianne sounded close to tears. "Do you wish me to warn him in some way? I could ride to meet him at the ferry and warn him away."

So Marianne wished to impress the dashing Frog, did she? Georgette savored the power of possession. "I cannot allow you to endanger yourself. Besides, how can I convince Mr. LaTournay of my faithfulness to him unless I betray the spy?"

"But, Gigi, Mr. Pringle has twenty-five men ready to seize the Frog tonight. They plan a public hanging."

Fear licked like flames at Georgette's confidence. What did Jean-Maurice plan to do? Only now did it occur to her to wonder why he planned to meet her in the orchard. Would he needlessly expose himself to danger? She shook her head. "He has always escaped their traps before. I pray he will find a way of escape tonight."

"I, too, will pray for his safety," Marianne whispered.

❧

Before he left the house at eleven that night, Pringle gave Georgette explicit instructions about when, where, and how she should leave the house and make her way to the orchard. "We will be watching you, and any deviation from the plan will cost you dearly." He narrowed his eyes. "Any hint of warning, and that Frog of yours takes twenty-five musket balls in his gut. *My* shot just might miss its target and find you."

"I understand."

Marianne and Georgette held hands and prayed while they waited for time to pass. Georgette heard running horses outside. Would Jean-Maurice be prepared for this unfriendly welcome? Surely he did not depend solely on the Grenville servants to protect him. Why bother coming at all? What ulterior motive directed his movements?

Several shots rang out. Men shouted. Horses neighed.

The women exchanged startled stares. Running to an upstairs bedroom window, Marianne and Georgette looked toward the Jamaica road, seeing torches and milling figures. Georgette's mother and Mrs. Grenville joined them.

"What has happened?" Mr. Grenville spoke from the doorway. Receiving no answer, he pushed his way to the window. "Something has gone awry. This disturbance would alert the enemy."

Calling for a servant, he stormed from the room and thundered downstairs. Out in the road, the torches moved slowly into the distance and disappeared from sight.

The women followed him, conjecturing among themselves. Georgette checked the grandfather clock in the front hall. Soon it would be her appointed time to meet the Frog in the orchard. Would the meeting ever take place?

A liveried man rushed through the front door, bent to gasp for breath with his hands on his knees, then ran into the parlor. The women followed him, hoping to overhear his news.

"What is it, Toby? Stop puffing and tell me what you have discovered," Mr. Grenville ordered.

The man struggled for breath. "I run clear from the crossroads, suh. Mr. Pringle's men, they was captured by a band of associators. They be taken back to New York City tonight. Mr. Pringle, he went crazy and shot the leader spy, the one he calls the Frog. Then somebody shot Mr. Pringle, but he ain't hurt bad. Somebody carried that Frogman off somewheres, but nobody knows what become of 'im or who he was."

fourteen

Neither is there salvation in any other: for there is none other name under heaven given among men, whereby we must be saved.
ACTS 4:12

Georgette lowered herself into a chair and laid her head back.

Dear Lord God, I beseech You to protect my husband and bring him home to me. Jean-Maurice believes he is doing right in Your eyes, I am certain. Forgive his unbelief and make Yourself known to him in an unmistakable way. Please make me worthy.

The Grenvilles and Georgette's parents discussed the subverted plan in hushed tones. Marianne brought Georgette a cup of chocolate and knelt at her feet, looking up with worried eyes. Georgette held her cup with one hand and reached to squeeze Marianne's hand with the other. "I am certain Mr. Pringle will recover. Toby's report indicated that he was not seriously injured."

"Yes, but the Frog." Tears turned Marianne's eyes into sparkling blue pools. "He was so brave and daring. No wonder you loved him. I wish such a man would take interest in me."

"You speak as though he were dead." Georgette snatched her hand back and sipped at her chocolate. "I do not believe it." The enormous lump in her throat could not be swallowed or ignored.

"I pray you are right." Marianne inspected her fidgeting fingers. "You say you never saw his face, yet you loved him. Did he ever kiss you, Georgette?"

Georgette lifted a brow. "How romantic you have become, Marianne. At first he only touched my hands, but his voice held a passion that set my soul aflame. He called me 'ma belle grenooj' or something like that."

Marianne's forehead wrinkled. " 'My beautiful frog'? But he was the Frog, not you. Are you certain he said *'grenouille'?*"

Georgette wanted to laugh and cry at once. The rogue! How dared he call her a frog! Setting down her chocolate, she rose with a rustle of petticoats to walk across the room. She covered her lips with one hand and propped her elbow with the other, her old habit. Did Jean-Maurice think her mouth too large? Or did he call her his frog because he had always intended her to be his mate—one frog admiring another?

Her thoughts flitted from one concern to another. Small wonder he had been secretive all these months of their marriage. Georgette recalled several instances when she had reviled Whig leaders and condemned the revolutionary forces. How could Jean-Maurice know that his wife loved him far more than she cared about politics? Whatever course he decided upon was the right choice as far as Georgette was concerned, knowing as she did that her husband would dedicate himself to no cause without careful deliberation.

In the wee hours of the morning, Georgette retired to her chamber and drew the curtains around the cold bed. Tonight she would receive no visit from an audacious frog. Still praying for her husband's safety and salvation, she drifted into sleep.

❧

Just past noon the following day, while Georgette sat knitting in the parlor in the company of her parents and the Grenvilles, the servant Toby burst into the room. "Mr. Grenville, suh!"

"What is it, Toby?" Mr. Grenville growled, looking up from his newspaper.

"Mr. LaTournay—he rides up the lane."

Georgette's father sat up, knocking his wig askew. "Ah! Hope returns with him." Casting a burning glare upon Georgette, he ordered, "You will do and say nothing to further alienate the man."

"Yes, Father." Georgette could scarcely conceal her elation. Her Frog was alive and well! Clasping her hands amid the folds of her gown, she strove to control her breathing. The lace ruffles upon her breast rose and fell much too violently. Staring at her lap, she reminded herself of the role she must play: the penitent wife.

The front door opened, voices sounded, and footsteps crossed the hall. Mr. LaTournay paused in the parlor doorway. Georgette took in a quick breath. Flawless attire and polished boots proclaimed him the fine gentleman, although a recalcitrant lock of hair dangled beside one of his high cheekbones. She resumed breathing with conscious effort.

"Welcome, LaTournay." Mr. Grenville bowed and offered a chair. "Your return signifies the return of hope to this household. You are no doubt aware of the attack upon our loyal citizens? Pringle has been taken captive. A dram of whiskey to dispel the chill?"

Mr. LaTournay bowed to the ladies, accepted the chair, and declined the drink. "Take heart. City leaders are already protesting the detainment of your townspeople. I doubt their incarceration will be of long duration. A more significant loss was the cache of gunpowder hidden in Mr. Johannes Smythe's barn. Had you heard of that calamity? The Whigs confiscated all."

"And Pringle's plot to capture that infamous Frog spy has been foiled," Mrs. Grenville added. "Do you think Mr. Pringle is badly injured?"

"I had not heard that his injury was severe. Some say he killed the Frog; others say the spy escaped unscathed." Mr. LaTournay held his hands to the fire, leaning his elbows upon his widespread knees. Georgette thought his face looked pale.

"A ship sails for England next week," her father said.

Mr. LaTournay studied his father-in-law dispassionately. "Whether or not you sail on that ship depends upon your daughter. I hear she took part in Pringle's plot to apprehend the spy. Was her participation voluntary? That is the pertinent question."

His enigmatic gaze turned upon Georgette. Despite her certainty, doubts assailed her. Jean-Maurice was the Frog. . . wasn't he? Could it be possible that he possessed a double, a twin? Who was this hostile stranger, after all?

"I–I wrote a note to bring the Frog here. It is not my fault that the plot failed."

His fixed stare brought heat to her face. "I shall never betray you, Mr. LaTournay," she added. Somewhere behind that forbidding mask must lurk her Jean-Maurice.

A sneer curled his lip. "Never—as long as I never turn my back upon you. We shall discuss this matter further in private." His voice held an ominous note. Georgette heard Marianne inhale sharply.

LaTournay rose. "Talbot, almost I am tempted to send your daughter back to England with you until this military conflict ends, but that would not serve my purposes. She will do penance at my pleasure. I shall purchase passage for you and Mrs. Talbot before my return north." He turned to Mrs. Grenville and Georgette's white-faced mother. "Pardon my blunt speech, ladies. Disillusionment brings out the worst in a man. I promise that my wife will suffer no physical harm, Mrs. Talbot; you need not fear."

Mrs. Grenville sputtered into speech. "You are always welcome to lodge here, Mr. LaTournay. The third-floor chamber still awaits your pleasure."

"I am grateful for your hospitality." His burning gaze once more focused upon Georgette. "Hence I shall retire until dinner. Mrs. LaTournay, you will accompany me."

Wilted beneath his stare, Georgette rose, excused herself, and led the way upstairs. As they passed into the front hall, her father's comment followed: "What that girl needs is a flogging. Her mother always pampered her. Deceitful, she is. No respect for authority."

Jean-Maurice said not a word as he followed Georgette up two flights and into her chamber. "Yours is the adjoining room," she said, but he closed her chamber door and leaned his back against it, eyes closed, chest heaving.

"Maybe tar and feathers were not too harsh after all," he mused aloud. "Almost I wish I had not already purchased his passage to England. Yet, for your mother's sake and to remove him from your vicinity, the fee was well spent."

Georgette regarded her husband from a distance, still uncertain. "You look pale, Jean-Maurice. Are you ill?"

"No, I am shot," he said softly.

"What? Where? Are you dying?" Georgette watched as he staggered over to collapse upon her bed. "Has a doctor seen your wound?"

"Pull off my boots, woman, and cease that incessant weeping!"

Georgette leaped to obey, trembling in surprise and hurt. Footsteps sounded in the room below, and a door closed.

After his boots hit the floor, Jean-Maurice smiled up at her. "Hush, *ma chérie*—speak softly. My injury must not be known. Pierre bound it and applied a poultice. The damage is not serious, I think. The ball entered my shoulder from the side and exited through the back. Pierre thinks it bounced off my shoulder blade. I have suffered worse injury in the past." He closed his eyes and sighed. "Pierre shot Pringle through the arm."

"You should have stayed in bed instead of riding over here today to play the angry husband," Georgette scolded, wiping tears from her face with the backs of her hands. She dipped a handkerchief in her basin, wrung it out, and placed it upon his forehead. "Do you have a fever? Do you need your bandage changed?" She bent to lay her cheek against his.

"At present I need only rest and you." His eyes opened. "I could not leave you to wonder if I were dead or alive. Now we are together, all will be well." He lifted his right arm in invitation. "Come and 'do penance at my pleasure.' Rest with me. You look peaked."

"Where is Pierre?" Georgette covered him with a blanket and slid in beside him. Her hoop skirt rose behind her, admitting a draft. She tried to push it down, to no avail.

Jean-Maurice smiled. "You will seldom see Pierre, but he is near. Like a guardian angel."

The question must be asked. "Will you ever tell me how you received that scar on your throat and why you have nightmares?"

A pause. "Some tales are best left untold."

"When I heard that you had been shot, I prayed for your safety, but mainly I wondered. . . Please tell me, Jean-Maurice: Had you died last night, what would have become of your soul?"

He squeezed her gently. "The angels would have carried me to the Holy City. Never fear."

"So you know that God has forgiven you?" Georgette lifted her head to get a clear look at his face.

His dark eyes glimmered at her from beneath their thick lashes, and a double chin formed as he tipped his face down. "I am forgiven for Christ's sake, not for any worth in myself. Like the apostle Peter, I at last came to realize that, short of inventing my own god and religion, I had no choice but to abandon my pride and accept God's gift."

"When did this happen? Why did you not tell me?" She crossed her hands over the solid muscles of his chest and rested her chin upon her fingers, trying to pretend her voice did not wobble with emotion. "What do you mean about Peter?"

"I would have told you sometime." He looked uncomfortable. "It happened gradually since our talk that night. I refer to the Gospel of John, chapter six. 'Then Simon Peter answered him, Lord, to whom shall we go? thou hast the words of eternal life. And we believe and are sure that thou art that Christ, the Son of the living God.' And also in the book of Acts chapter four: 'There is none other name given among men by which we must be saved.' Jesus Christ is my Lord and my God, and I shall serve Him all my days. That is all."

Georgette hid her face against his broad chest and wept. "Oh, thank God, thank God! Jean-Maurice, I love you so."

❧

If the Talbots and Grenvilles wondered about the amount of time Georgette and Jean-Maurice spent upstairs, they made no comment. Pierre's prompt attention to the injury and Jean-Maurice's iron constitution collaborated toward quick healing. Georgette winced at the holes and bruises marring her husband's skin, but she rejoiced at his uneventful recovery. She hid away the soiled bandages until Pierre could collect and wash them for her. Each night the nimble servant availed himself of Jean-Maurice's entry—the gable window.

Although her husband slept much of the time, he dressed carefully for meals. No one could possibly have guessed at his injury. He conversed with the men about current affairs, rejoiced at rumors of the captive farmers' imminent release, and chuckled at her father's jokes concerning the pitiful Continental Army. To Georgette, he maintained in public a polite, guarded behavior.

After four days of rest, Jean-Maurice decided he was strong enough to travel home, overruling Georgette's protests. "All reports indicate that the Hudson is still open. I am well enough to ride in a boat. I weary of this house and these people, and we should depart before Pringle's return."

The morning of their departure, Pierre loaded their trunks upon a cart and brought a new pair of hired horses. Georgette kept a worried eye on her husband during their travel preparations, but Jean-Maurice showed no sign of weakness.

Marianne drew her aside in the hallway. Georgette returned her friend's hug, feeling guilty for the lack of attention she had given her. Marianne's blue eyes brimmed. "I shall miss you, Gigi. I see the wary glances you give your husband, but truly

I believe you need not fear. When he thinks no one is looking, Mr. LaTournay still gazes upon you with affection. Your marriage can be saved if you set your mind to forget about the Frog and strive to become a submissive wife. I shall pray for your complete reconciliation with Mr. LaTournay."

Humbled and slightly amused, Georgette bowed her head and squeezed Marianne's hands. "Thank you, my dear. I shall pray that God will bring a great love into your life—a man worthy of you." She kissed Marianne's soft cheek.

Her mother waylaid her next. "Dearest girl, I am so thankful your husband purchased our passage instead of simply giving Mr. Talbot the money. He is so generous and kind." She leaned close and lowered her voice. "He gave me extra money in case of another emergency; your father does not know. Do try to value Mr. LaTournay and forget that dreadful Frog. He is handsome from some angles, and I believe he cares for you. How distinguished he is! Do you not think his eyes are fine?"

Georgette restrained a smile. "Very fine, indeed. He has been kind and patient with me this week, Mummy, despite his harsh words. I believe I do care for him, after all. Our home in the north is lovely; I wish you could see it. I anticipate our homecoming with pleasure." She found it difficult to restrict her speech to such glaring understatements.

"I am gratified to hear it. Although your marriage was arranged, it does not necessarily follow that it cannot be felicitous."

They linked arms and entered the front hallway where the others waited. "This time I shall make certain they sail with the ship," Mr. Grenville was saying in a hearty tone. "You can count on me."

"I do, sir," Mr. LaTournay returned with a respectful bow. He shook her father's hand and accepted her mother's embrace. Georgette wondered if he was remembering the last "final" farewell. Despite her cynical thoughts, she wept once again while hugging her mother.

As they rode side-by-side along the ferry road, Jean-Maurice reached across the intervening space and grasped Georgette's hand. "Are you sorry to take leave of your parents?"

Georgette pondered the question and sighed. "Somewhat. I long to be home again with you. And Caramel."

"Ah, yes, that love offering from my rival, *le Grenouille.*"

His harsh tone startled Georgette until she caught the twinkle in his eye. "A little uncertainty would do you good," she returned. "And I am reminded to inquire why you call me your frog. Marianne translated for me." Her irritation increased when he laughed aloud. "Do I resemble a frog? Does my large mouth amuse you?"

He caught her mount's reins and stopped both horses. "*Ma épouse chérie*, can you believe that I find anything about you objectionable? In my eyes, you are altogether lovely. I behold your lips to think of only one thing."

Putting his weight in his left stirrup, he leaned over to kiss her. Smiling, he returned to his seat and released her horse. "Now that we have scandalized the populace of Queens, shall we proceed?"

Swallowing hard, Georgette nodded. The joy in her heart must have glowed on her face, for every time Jean-Maurice looked her way that entire day, he smiled.

fifteen

And the angel of the LORD appeared unto him, and said unto him,
The LORD is with thee, thou mighty man of valour.
JUDGES 6:12

Firelight flickered on the oak beams and plaster walls of Georgette's bedchamber. A log fell in a shower of sparks. Jean-Maurice rose to brush the hot ashes away from Caramel's basket and rebuild the fire. Straightening, he flexed his shoulders and glanced up to meet Georgette's gaze.

"Does it ache?" she asked.

"Not too badly." He sat down across from her.

"What will you do after you are fully recovered, Jean-Maurice?" Georgette rose to stand behind his chair and rub his shoulders. Six weeks after the shooting, he had regained much of his former strength, though he had not yet regained full mobility in his left arm. He used it to toss a ball for Caramel. The little dog pounced on the toy and brought it back.

"I am uncertain." Jean-Maurice picked up the slimy ball and threw it again. "Because my identity yet remains unknown, my superiors wish me to organize further counterintelligence operations. British spies are everywhere. If we intend to win this war, we must fight fire with fire. I have also been requested to train regular troops in the art of bayonet warfare."

"You would fight in this war?" Georgette tried to sound brave.

"I had hoped never again to join in combat."

"Again? You have fought before?"

Silence. Caramel dropped the ball at Jean-Maurice's feet and woofed for attention. Jean-Maurice obliged by throwing the ball, but his thoughts were obviously elsewhere.

"Did you fight in the Indian wars? Is that what happened when your father returned for you? And you must have fought on the side of the French. But you were only a boy at the time!"

His shoulders tightened. Georgette watched him run one finger up the scar from his collar to his chin. "My childhood ended the day my father came to this house. In the name of war, I have committed atrocities of which I can never speak. As a spy, I was obliged to accept the reputation of a womanizer and pretend to woo another man's wife, a mistake that nearly cost me all I hold dear. Mere words cannot express the remorse I suffered when you scorned my suit."

"I recall the Frog defending your reputation to me," Georgette said in an attempt to lighten his mood.

He shook his head. "Yet you believed me an immoral man even after our marriage, being too innocent yourself to recognize my inexperience with women. I deserved your suspicion, for I had deceived you, lied to you. For all this evil, God has forgiven me, just as you said He would. But how can I fight another war or engage in further intelligence work, knowing I may be obliged to repeat sins of my past?"

Georgette kissed the top of his head. "You would not repeat the past, because now you belong to God. The torment that once burned in your eyes is gone; God's peace fills you."

He caught her hand and brought it to his cheek. "Georgette, you are God's wondrous gift to me. I do not deserve you." His broken whisper brought tears to her eyes.

"Neither do I deserve you. I know it is difficult for you to speak of your past, but it helps me to understand you better. Whatever comes in our future, Jean-Maurice, I want to enjoy each moment we spend together so that I shall have no regrets. We are one now, and I shall endeavor to assist in any task the Lord assigns you, whether it is to spy for the Whigs or to fight for their army."

He pulled her into his lap and buried his face in her loose hair. "Woman, if ever I conceal my activities from you again, rest assured that I think only of your safety. I trust you completely. In the past you have been my unwitting accomplice; now you are my mate in every sense."

Their future loomed cloudy and uncertain, yet Georgette's heart was at peace. "One *bonne grenouille* deserves another. Um, Jean-Maurice, how does one say 'tadpole' in French?"

"*Tetard.* Why?"

Georgette merely smiled.

A Letter To Our Readers

Dear Reader:

In order that we might better contribute to your reading enjoyment, we would appreciate your taking a few minutes to respond to the following questions. We welcome your comments and read each form and letter we receive. When completed, please return to the following:

Fiction Editor
Heartsong Presents
PO Box 719
Uhrichsville, Ohio 44683

1. Did you enjoy reading *Faithful Traitor* by Jill Stengl?
   - ❑ Very much! I would like to see more books by this author!
   - ❑ Moderately. I would have enjoyed it more if

   ____

   ____

   ____

2. Are you a member of **Heartsong Presents**? ❑ Yes ❑ No
   If no, where did you purchase this book? ________________

   ____

3. How would you rate, on a scale from 1 (poor) to 5 (superior), the cover design? ______________________

4. On a scale from 1 (poor) to 10 (superior), please rate the following elements.

____ Heroine	____ Plot
____ Hero	____ Inspirational theme
____ Setting	____ Secondary characters

5. These characters were special because?________________

____

____

6. How has this book inspired your life?________________

____

____

7. What settings would you like to see covered in future **Heartsong Presents** books? ________________

____

____

8. What are some inspirational themes you would like to see treated in future books? ________________

____

____

9. Would you be interested in reading other **Heartsong Presents** titles? ❑ Yes ❑ No

10. Please check your age range:

❑ Under 18	❑ 18-24
❑ 25-34	❑ 35-45
❑ 46-55	❑ Over 55

Name____________________________________

Occupation ________________________________

Address __________________________________

City______________ State______ Zip__________